Mirror of the Invisible World

MIRROR OF THE INVISIBLE WORLD

Tales from the *Khamseh* of Nizami

PETER J. CHELKOWSKI
Department of Near Eastern Languages and Literatures · New York University

WITH AN ESSAY BY PRISCILLA P. SOUCEK
Department of the History of Art · University of Michigan

FOREWORD BY RICHARD ETTINGHAUSEN
Department of Islamic Art · The Metropolitan Museum of Art

THE METROPOLITAN MUSEUM OF ART · NEW YORK

ON THE COVER: a decorative leather inside cover from the original binding of the manuscript

FRONTISPIECE: detail of Miniature 11, *Bahram Gur in the Sandalwood Pavilion*

Publication of this book has been made possible in part by contributions provided by His Excellency Youssef Khoshkish, President of the Melli Bank, Teheran, Iran, through the generous agency of Mr. Ralph E. Becker, President of the Iran-American Society of the United States, who also contributed to the publication.

The texts of "Khosrow and Shirin," "Layla and Majnun," and "The Seven Princesses" are adapted, in part, from the *Tales of the Khamsa* as retold by Vernon Newton from the transcriptions of Peter Chelkowski. By permission of Vernon Newton.

Book designed by Peter Oldenburg
Photography by William F. Pons
Engraved and printed by Conzett + Huber AG, Zurich, Switzerland
Published 1975
All rights reserved by The Metropolitan Museum of Art, New York
Printed in Switzerland

LIBRARY OF CONGRESS CATALOGING IN PUBLICATION DATA

Chelkowski, Peter J.
   Mirror of the invisible world.

   "Published on the occasion of the opening of the new Islamic Galleries at the Metropolitan Museum of Art."
CONTENTS: Khosrow and Shirin.—Layla and Majnun.—The Seven Princesses.
   1. Nizami Ganjavi, 1140 or 41-1202 or 3—Manuscripts—Addresses, essays, lectures. I. Nizami Ganjavi, 1140 or 41-1202 or 3. Khamseh. II. New York (City). Metropolitan Museum of Art. III. Title.

PZ4.C516Mi   [PS3553.H3488]   813'.5'4   75-28305   ISBN 0-87099-142-6

CONTENTS

FOREWORD	vii
PREFACE AND ACKNOWLEDGMENTS	ix
INTRODUCTION	1
THE *KHAMSEH* OF 1524/25	11
Khosrow and Shirin	21
Layla and Majnun	49
The Seven Princesses	69
OTHER IMPORTANT KNOWN MANUSCRIPTS OF THE *KHAMSEH*	116

FOREWORD

Next to Ferdowsi's *Shah-nameh*, the *Khamseh* or "Quintet" of Nizami offered the best opportunity for a wide-ranging series of illustrations to the Iranian miniaturist. Although these paintings lacked the typical iconographic formulas of the epic—heroic subjects such as enthronements, battles of whole armies, duels of the paladins, and encounters with demons and monsters—they depicted instead many scenes of great variety and romantic appeal. These have been rendered in innumerable manuscripts from the late fourteenth century up to the nineteenth century and have resulted in some of the most beloved motifs of Iranian pictorial arts. The scenes of Khosrow discovering Shirin bathing in a pool of water, of Shirin visiting Farhad as he carves his way through the mountain of Bisutun, of the unhappy sculptor carrying his queen and her horse on his shoulders, of Layla and her boy lover in school, of the poet Majnun in the desert surrounded by wild and tame animals, of Bahram Gur in the brilliantly colored pavilions of his seven beautiful princesses, are well known to all admirers of Iranian art in both the East and the West.

While the basic iconography of these scenes developed in the late fourteenth and in the fifteenth century, some of the finest versions date from the sixteenth century and their influence has been long-lasting. Just as Nizami's poems have served as models to many other poets in Iran, India, and Turkey, so have the illustrations of the original five poems been followed by the miniaturists illuminating later versions. Indeed, so popular are these subjects that they are found not only as illustrations of manuscripts but also as pictorial themes on tiles, chests, pen cases, textiles, and even carpets.

Aside from the better-known scenes, there are others which illustrate different episodes, frequently of a minor character. To understand these fully, it is necessary to be familiar with the varied subjects and themes of the poems, especially the major ones. Happily, this is now possible as a result of the investigations of Professor Peter J. Chelkowski, of New York University, who has written an English adaptation of the tales from Nizami's *Khamseh*. He has provided, in addition, an introduction and commentaries on each story which not only present the historical background but also give us an insight into the rich imagination of the twelfth-century poet.

The publication of this volume coincides with the opening of the newly installed Islamic Galleries in The Metropolitan Museum of Art. The new galleries enable us to exhibit a very rich collection in a full and systematic fashion for the first time in many decades and provide us with a special opportunity to display the Museum's wealth of miniature painting. The Museum owns, among other Nizami manuscripts, one of the key manuscripts of the early fifteenth century, written and painted for one of the greatest of Iranian bibliophiles, the Timurid prince Baysonghor, residing in Herat, and one of the finest early sixteenth-century manuscripts painted in the same city. It is the miniatures from the latter, dated 1524/25 and one of the most sumptuous manuscripts ever produced in Persia, that illustrate this volume.

This new presentation of Nizami's stories, together with their splendid classical illustrations, enhanced by Professor Priscilla P. Soucek's art-historical introduction, should go far in recapturing the appeal that this art exerted for so many centuries on the Persian-speaking world.

RICHARD ETTINGHAUSEN
Consultative Chairman
Department of Islamic Art
The Metropolitan Museum of Art

PREFACE AND ACKNOWLEDGMENTS

Persian poetry, like Persian art, tends to be decorative, ornamental, and graceful. Apart from depth of feeling, a poet's originality often lies in the refinement of his moods, in his play on words, his subtle allusions, and his mastery of the rhythms and cadences of the language. Many Persian poems, especially epics, are more leisurely paced and considerably longer than those with which Western readers are familiar; indeed, they seem exotic to Western ears, and are appreciated and understood mainly by linguists and scholars in the field. This is unfortunate, for in Persian poetry, and especially in the *Khamseh* of Nizami, there is much to delight an American audience.

In this volume three stories from the *Khamseh*—"Khosrow and Shirin," "Layla and Majnun," and "The Seven Princesses"—have been retold in prose for the contemporary reader. And since a direct translation of the *Khamseh* would result in nearly sixty thousand lines, or some fifteen hundred pages, the stories have been abridged in the retelling. We hope to be forgiven by the specialists for taking these liberties; indeed, we have taken them in an attempt to present Nizami's wonderful tales as living literature and to convey in them the spirit of the poet. With this in mind, we have avoided the use of diacritical marks wherever possible and have simplified the transliteration of foreign words.

There are many persons whose invaluable assistance I gratefully acknowledge. Dr. Richard Ettinghausen, Consultative Chairman of the Department of Islamic Art at The Metropolitan Museum of Art, has been a constant source of inspiration and encouragement. Marie Lukens Swietochowski, Associate Curator, has helped me unstintingly at every turn. Margot Feely and Shari Lewis of the Publications Department took great pains with the editing and production of this book.

My special thanks go to Vernon Newton for his unflagging cooperation and for his gracious willingness to allow me to borrow freely from his interpretations of the stories. I am indebted to Priscilla Soucek for her searching analysis of the Metropolitan Museum's 1524/25 *Khamseh* from the art-historical perspective. Cynthia Philip brought her masterly and incisive editorial skills to the manuscript, and Charles Beardsley gave me many hints and much help in the initial translation of the *Khamseh*.

Finally, I note with great pleasure that this volume is being published on the occasion of the opening of the new Islamic Galleries at The Metropolitan Museum of Art. I congratulate the Metropolitan Museum; surely the new installation of the Museum's extensive and outstanding Islamic collection will stimulate the already increasing interest in Islamic art.

Peter J. Chelkowski
Department of Near Eastern
Languages and Literatures
New York University

INTRODUCTION

The beauty of the *Khamseh* of Nizami is unsurpassed in Persian literature. Sensuous, dramatic, gracious, and refined, these epic poems display Nizami's genius for linguistic invention and psychological characterization—a talent imitated by hundreds of poets since his time, but never equaled.

Written during the last thirty years of the twelfth century A. D., the *Khamseh*[1] consists of five long poems or *masnavis*.[2] The first is "The Treasury of Mysteries," a didactico-philosophical-mystical treatise. The remaining four—"Khosrow and Shirin," "Layla and Majnun," "The Seven Princesses," and "Alexander the Great"—are romances. Both the form and content of these poems constitute a breakthrough in Persian poetry which, until Nizami, found its most perfect expression in the more limited heroic genre, the sonnet, panegyric ode, or quatrain.[3]

The culture of Nizami's Persia is renowned for its deep-rooted tradition and splendor. In pre-Islamic times, it had developed extraordinarily rich and exact means of expression in music, architecture, and daily life as well as in writing, and although Iran, its center—or, as the poets believed, its heart—was continually overrun by invading armies and immigrants, this tradition was always able to absorb, transform, and ultimately overcome foreign intrusion. Alexander the Great was only one of many conquerors to be seduced by the Persian way of life.

This preeminence persisted and, indeed, was increased with the advent of Islam, for Persian culture played a vital role in the Eastern caliphate, which borrowed Persian forms of administration and government. In the seventh and eighth centuries, when other Near and Middle Eastern languages were disappearing under the onslaught of the Arab-Islamic invasion, the Persian language continued to develop. By the end of the tenth century, Persian literature was world renowned; it was heralded from the eastern Mediterranean to the banks of the Indus.

When the classical Islamic Empire began to disintegrate in the ninth century A. D., Persian culture continued to influence the court life of many rulers, even in areas remote from the Iranian plateau. In fact, many government administrators were of Persian origin.

Under the great Seljuq Turkish dynasty, although Persian political power was restricted, Persian culture reached new heights of achievement. Poetry was nourished by the vigorous, competitive patronage of the local rulers and the office of court poet was coveted; it was during the Seljuq period that Omar Khayyam composed his famous quatrains or *ruba'yyats*. Architecture, based on exquisitely intricate brickwork, was noble, powerful, and structurally sophisticated. Textiles and pottery were elegant and imaginative. Educational institutions expanded.

During the last quarter of the twelfth century, when Nizami began his *Khamseh*, Seljuq supremacy was on the decline and political unrest and social ferment were increasing. However, Persian culture characteristically flourished when political power was diffused rather than centralized, and so Persian remained the primary language, Persian civil servants were in great demand, Persian merchants were successful, and princedoms continued to vie for the services of Persian poets. This was especially true in Ganjeh, the Caucasian outpost town where Nizami lived. According to literary historians, Ganjeh was a major center of cultural activity. During the Seljuq period it boasted at least seven important poets writing odes, panegyrics, and satiric, lyric, and epic poetry.

Of these, Nizami was unique. His work is a synthesis of Persian literary achievements up to his time—the heroicness of Ferdowsi, the fatalism of Khayyam, the humanism of Sana'i, the lyricism of Unsuri and Farrukhi, and the eroticism of Gurgani. Nizami enlarged this rich and varied tradition with contemporary mysticism, with his encyclopedic knowledge, and with his sublime poetic gift. The breadth of his thought and the beauty and invention of his imagery are still without equal. The fourteenth-century master poet Hafiz wrote of his work: "This Ancient Vault contains nothing beneath it comparable for the beauty to the words of Nizami."

Few facts about the life of Nizami are certain. Because he was not a court poet and it was his poetry rather than his life or his political connections that won him enduring fame, he does not appear in the annals of the dynasties, which list the names and events of ruling families and eminent persons. *Tazkerehs*, the compilations of Near and Middle Eastern literary memoirs that include verses and maxims of the great poets along with biographical information and commentary on their styles, refer to him only briefly and, since much of the material is based on legend, anecdote, and hearsay, must be used with caution.

By far the best source of information on Nizami's life is the *Khamseh* itself, for it contains much autobiographical material. However, this, too, must be scrutinized critically; many verses attributed to Nizami are disputed as interpolations of later writers and copyists. The earliest extant version of the *Khamseh* dates from 1362,[4] some one hundred and fifty years after the death of the poet; contemporary manuscripts disappeared or were destroyed during the Mongol invasions.

It is believed that Nizami[5] was born around 535 A. H. / 1140 A. D. in the Caucasian town of Ganjeh, now the city of Kirovabad in the Soviet republic of

Azarbaijan. This crossroads town was a beehive of diverse peoples, languages, and religions. In spite of the fact that traveling was easy, Nizami rarely left its precincts—he once called himself the "Prisoner of Ganjeh." Although he wrote in the postscript of "Khosrow and Shirin" that he went some distance from the town to a fete given in his honor by Atabeg Qizil Arslan, it should be noted that, exact in other matters, Nizami's geography was never very accurate.

Nizami's father was from a devout Muslim tradition, and it is believed he may have been a civil servant who migrated from the province of Qum in North Central Iran.[6] He was quite probably well-off, for although Nizami was orphaned in childhood, he received an excellent education. From his poetry it is evident that he was learned in mathematics, astronomy, medicine, jurisprudence, and philosophy as well as in music and the arts.

Nizami married three times, but despite Muslim law, which permits polygamy, he was monogamous. The wife he loved most was his first, the Kipchak slave Afaq, presented to him by a ruler of Darband as a token of his appreciation for the initial poem of the *Khamseh*, "The Treasury of Mysteries." Instead of keeping her as a concubine, Nizami married her, and she bore him his only child, a son, Muhammad, who became as dear to him as "the light to his eyes." Many passages in the last four poems of the *Khamseh* are devoted to precepts for Muhammad's ethical and intellectual instruction. The lofty character of Shirin, heroine of the second *masnavi* of the *Khamseh*, was undoubtedly modeled after Afaq. Her untimely death is sentimentally regarded by some scholars as a sacrifice to Nizami's artistic deity for the completion of "Khosrow and Shirin"; others regard it more likely as the inspiration behind the story. Of his other wives little is known, although their premature deaths, each coinciding with the completion of an epic, are also interpreted as sacrifices, even by Nizami himself, who, if the verses are genuine, cried out in anguish, "God, why is it that for every *masnavi* I must sacrifice a wife!"

Researchers and biographers differ by thirty-seven years as to the date of Nizami's death (575 A. H. / 1180 A. D. to 613 A. H. / 1217 A. D.), but since it is certain he was writing the *Khamseh* until at least 1200 A. D., the earlier date must be disregarded. So beloved are his poems that his tomb has been a place of devoted pilgrimage for over seven centuries, and he was given the honorific title of Hakim, or learned doctor.

The character of Nizami is less obscure than the facts of his life, for unlike most other poets of his time, he did not conceal his thoughts, beliefs, and emotions. Spontaneity is his special magic. So profound and complex are his feelings and observations, however, that they are susceptible to many interpretations, especially because of his use of dazzling imagery, extended metaphor, and unbridled fantasy.

Nizami was a true renaissance man, even a social reformer. He refused the position of court poet so that he could retain independence both of belief and of artistic expression. He was democratic, delineating simple people with as much insight and compassion as his heroes. Artisans were particularly dear to him. Painters, sculptors, architects, and musicians are carefully portrayed and often play crucial roles. In the romance "Khosrow and Shirin," the artistic accomplishments and the loyalty of the painter Shapur and the devotion and engineering feats of Farhad create a far more lasting impression than do the errant adventures of the titular hero, King Khosrow. The details with which Nizami describes musicians are one of the delights of the *Khamseh* and make it a principal source of our present knowledge of twelfth-century Persian musical composition and instruments. However, in spite of his interest in commoners, Nizami did not reject the institution of kingship; he always believed it was an integral and sacred part of the Persian way of life.

It was particularly in his treatment of women that Nizami broke with the custom of his times. In life, women were generally treated as chattel; in poetry, as mere decoration. The heroic epics, even of the immortal Ferdowsi, celebrate the exploits of men, be it in war or in love. The action is man to man, and the thought is of men about men; men are raised to the level of supermen. But in Nizami it is the women who are strong, subtle, and virtuous, and, at the same time, tender, passionate, and enchantingly beautiful; they have sharp, educated intellects. In "Layla and Majnun," boys and girls study in the same classroom from the same master, and in other romances women are depicted as excelling in horsemanship and marksmanship. But because Nizami always exhibits both sides of the coin, his women are also arrogant, deceitful, cantankerous, vacillating, lonely, and despondent. Nizami's fascination with women and his elevation of their estate immeasurably enriches the psychological content of his *Khamseh;* and it is certainly one of the elements that has made his poetic achievement so enduring. In contrast to the ambiguity of Persian Sufi lyric poetry, Nizami's work is without a trace of homosexuality; his love relationships are always clearly heterosexual.

Intensifying Nizami's human interest in all people is his fierce passion for justice. Again and again, episodes and stories emphasize that it is the king's first duty to rule his people wisely, to protect them from wanton cruelty, to help them in time of natural disaster, and to create a government under which they can flourish spiritually as well as materially. He must carefully choose his advisers for their diligence and honesty. Nizami knew that reliance on corrupt administrators corrupts the king himself and does irreparable harm to his people.

To what extent Nizami's social sensitivity was based on his religious piety has long been of great interest to scholars. Many claim that he was a Sufi mystic.

Certainly there was a strong undercurrent of mysticism in Nizami's time and Sufi poetry reached its zenith then, but his name does not appear in the biographies of the Shaykhs, or mystic leaders. It is within the range of possibility, however, that he was attracted to the Akhi movement. This was a brotherhood, active among the artisans and craftsmen of the rapidly growing towns, which was devoted to works of social welfare. Its adherents did not reject this life, but sought to better it. The guild of architects, masons, and artists required a mystic initiation, and its teaching instruction and apprenticeship involved the mystic concept of unity through shape, color, and number. Nizami, whose interest in architecture, architectural decoration, and closeness to artisans are apparent in his poetry, could very well have been intimate with its members and influenced by them.

There are strains of bitterness and fatalism in Nizami's *masnavis*. He believed that in every life there is a crisis, something that cannot be undone and that molds all subsequent action—in his own life it was perhaps Afaq's love and her death. Part is due to external forces and part to inner individual forces. Nizami was strongly attracted to astrology, perceiving man as master of his fate only to a limited degree. This belief in the inconstancy of the world and the inevitability of the course of events are no doubt Sufi mystic themes and, therefore, support those claims that he was a Sufi mystic. But although Nizami's poetry does have mystic overtones, it is more an earth-bound mysticism in which renunciation of the body is in the mode of orthodox Islam, the getting rid of destructive desires so that a more perfect life can be led, rather than the shedding of the self for union with God.

Nizami is a humanist and a romantic first and last; his moralism and asceticism are always of this world, for although virtue always wins out, Nizami is happiest when he has a firm foundation on material and erotic pleasures. Nizami gloried in the extravagant splendors of princely gardens and courts—the perfumes, the silks, the jewels, the flamboyant colors—and appreciation of them was an integral part of his dedication to life in its totality.

Nizami's innate philosophy, nevertheless, is one of rational moderation. Although innovative, he never takes an extreme position. His abiding interest in the world around him, the heterogeneity of daily life in Ganjeh, his passionate interest in nature, and his training in history, mathematics, astronomy, medicine, and the philosophies of Greece and India made him a man of reason, a pragmatist, and a universalist.

One of the most comprehensive descriptions of Nizami's personality is given by the great English orientalist E. G. Browne: "And if his genius has few rivals amongst the poets of Persia, his character has even fewer. He was genuinely pious, yet singularly devoid of fanaticism and intolerance, self-respecting and independent, yet gentle and unostentatious, a loving father and husband. In a word, he may be justly described as combining lofty genius and blameless character in a degree unequaled by any other Persian poet."[7]

Nizami's strong character, his social sensibility, and his poetic genius fused with his rich Persian cultural heritage to create a new standard of literary achievement. Using themes from the oral tradition and written historical records, his poems unite pre-Islamic and Islamic Persia. Written in the *masnavi* poetic form, each line consists of two rhyming distichs independent of the other lines, similar to the doublet in Chaucer's *Canterbury Tales*. This form had long been used for narrative heroic and didactic poems, but through the imaginative artistry of Nizami it gained a splendor and flexibility never before achieved.

The first of the five poems is a didactico-philosophical-mystical work called "Makhzan al-Asrar," or "The Treasury of Mysteries." In this epic Nizami established a pattern for the introductory chapters of his later *masnavis* and for almost all *masnavis* written thereafter. They include verses in worship of God, followed by a chapter of praise and veneration of the prophet Muhammad and a description of Muhammad's ascension to the heavens. Then comes a prayer for the author, praise of the ruler, a chapter relating why the poem was created, and, finally, a chapter on the excellence of the literary word.

Nizami also ended each *masnavi* with a postscript. As well as commenting on the main theme of the poem, Nizami would use these chapters to defend his position and praise his benefactors or prospective benefactors. He also found them an appropriate place to counsel the reader or his son Muhammad.

Although the prince of Darband admired "The Treasury of Mysteries" so much that he presented Nizami with the slave girl Afaq, it apparently was not generally well-received. In his second major work, "Khosrow and Shirin," Nizami turned from mystical philosophy to historical romance. Its introduction records his cynicism toward public opinion as well as his desire to be acclaimed:

> Possessing a treasure like my "Makhzan al-Asrar"
> Why should I bother myself with romances?
> In today's world, however, there is no one
> Who hasn't a passion for romances.

"Khosrow and Shirin" proved to be a literary turning point not only for Nizami but for all of Persian poetry. Its dazzling use of language reached new heights; its emphasis on human rather than heroic elements and its intense delineation of the inner life of a broad range of characters were entirely original. Furthermore, it was the first poem in Persian literature to achieve complete structural and artistic unity.

In "Khosrow and Shirin," Nizami reveals himself a master dramatist. The plot is carefully constructed to enhance the story's psychological complexity; the characters work and grow under the stress of action to discover things about themselves and others and to make swift decisions. The tension of their interaction is sometimes almost insupportable, but the passion and fluency of the dialogue matches the flow of dramatic events. The animals, plants, and stars; the sunrises, sunsets, and the gloom of night are so vividly described that they, too, become a dramatic force in the story. Even music is used, not only for its own beauty but to heighten the drama. It is perhaps fortunate that Nizami was not a playwright, for he was not forced to limit his action in space and could make all the world, known and unknown, his stage. Unconfined by time, he could present the entire lifespan of his protagonists, following them even beyond the grave into paradise.

Some scholars hold that Nizami changed to the romantic genre to become popular, others because a patron so commissioned him. But it is also widely believed that he wrote "Khosrow and Shirin" as a tribute to his beloved wife Afaq. The work is technically so profoundly innovative, its human insights so penetrating, that it would seem that only an event of great personal significance —like Afaq's death—could have inspired it.

In his next romance, "Layla and Majnun," Nizami further perfected his dramatic gifts. "Layla and Majnun" is on a less heroic scale than "Khosrow and Shirin." The protagonists are not an historical king and queen, but rather a mad poet and his gentle, warm, and long-suffering beloved. The contrast between Majnun's desert—its storms, its sunsets, its nights, and its befriending beasts—and the civilized life of his beloved Layla is a triumph of poetic craftsmanship.

"The Seven Princesses" celebrates love as a serious pastime. Its elaborate exploration of all the facets of sensuality make it the most erotic of Nizami's works. But the eroticism is tempered by moralism. The spirit, as well as the senses, is aroused, leading to metaphorical transcendental love. In mysticism, to which Nizami was strongly attracted, love sublimated is one of the paths to God. Carnal love experienced through the exaltation of the senses is not condemned; instead it is relegated to its proper perspective as one of the harmonious elements of human life.

Always fascinated by the work of Ferdowsi, it was Nizami's goal in life to write an heroic epic of the same stature. And so, for his last long poem, Nizami chose as his theme the story of Alexander the Great, which is recounted in Ferdowsi's *Shah-nameh*. But although he considered "Alexander the Great" his most important work—and it contains some unrivaled passages—it fails to live up to the tight structural unity of "Khosrow and Shirin," "Layla and Majnun," and "The Seven Princesses." Nizami was too much of a humanist to deal effectively with an idealized hero; he had to make Alexander a person with doubts and frailties as well as god-like virtues and strengths.

Nizami's brilliance as a storyteller and dramatist is matched only by the brilliance of his language. It has an elaborate, bejeweled splendor; it swirls with color and chiaroscuro; at the same time, it has elegant purity and formality. And although it is often exaggerated, it is also extremely subtle. Nizami's capacity for precise psychological and physical description is extraordinary. The simple events of daily life are as vividly portrayed as are the opulent court banquets and royal hunts, which he so dearly loved. He had a genius for lucid and vigorous ornamentation.

Not only did Nizami introduce new metaphors and images; he also coined new words. By combining and playing with words and their meanings, he created fresh expressions and figures of speech. It can be said that Nizami was not only a painter with words, but a sculptor or architect, who, using simple bricks as his medium, builds palaces of breathtaking color, form, and intricacy.

H. Blochmann, the author of *The Prosody of the Persians,* says in his appraisal of Nizami's contribution to the Persian language: "...the poetry of the pre-classical period is full of ancient words and forms, licenses and irregularities in language, metre, and rhyme. These irregularities disappear with Nizami at the commencement of the classical period. Nizami is the classical poet of Persia par excellence. He reduced the numbers of licenses, purified the rhyme, the metre and the language, and expelled ancient words and forms. Even his *masnavis*—that form of poetry in which poets are allowed a greater freedom of expression—are eminently pure. He has been correctly called the Imam of Persian poetry."[8]

But this does not mean that Nizami's language is simple; on the contrary. C. E. Wilson, who first translated "The Seven Princesses" into English in 1924, wrote that Nizami "employs images and metaphors to which there is no key save in the possession of the poetic sense and of sound judgment.... His thoughts are deeper, his expression is more trenchant, crisp, and epigrammatic, though perhaps often more studied and artificial and generally more obscure and subtle."[9] The rising sun is a "yellow rose," and at sunset it is the "exquisite ruby being devoured by the exhausted phoenix"; when the phoenix, the world, has swallowed the ruby, it is then night. The stars are called "the narcissus" of the night, or they are "eye-sellers"; the world, as well as "the exhausted phoenix," is "the village," "the bridge," or the "little chest."

The sensuousness of Nizami's imagery is almost irresistible; but compelling, too, is its refinement. The tension between the fantasy and the purity of his expression mirrors perfectly the tension between the eroticism and the asceticism of his plots. Nizami is like a magical ice-skater who, within a set range of figures, performs ever more varied and exquisite arabesques until he mesmerizes the beholder.

Probably no Persian writer has inspired succeeding generations of poets more than Nizami. More than Ferdowsi or Hafiz, he became the model for poets of all languages from the western Mediterranean to East Asia; the stories from his *Khamseh* continue as models even today.

His dramatic, kaleidoscopic descriptions have had an equally great impact on artists. Nizami's passion for painting and decoration and the important role that artists play in all his epics have been a constant source of inspiration. The interaction of art and literature is a recurring theme in his works; and in "The Seven Princesses" it reaches extraordinary heights. A. J. Arberry, British scholar of Near Eastern civilizations and translator and interpreter of its literature, says of Nizami's romances: "Besides being excellent reading in themselves, [they] shared with the *Shah-nameh* the honor of supplying Persia's miniature painters with rich material for the exercise of their craft: the conjunction of glittering verse with brilliant art gave birth to some of the world's most splendid books."[10]

Nizami was conscious of his gifts and used them with joy and deliberation. Poets, he said, are the "princes of words." "Poetry is the mirror of what is visible, and what is invisible... the curtain of mystery, the shadow of the prophetic veil." "The temple of poetry was built by me," he declared, "and the art of poetry has been freed from earthly bounds.... All beings, young and old, have been excited by the magic of my words."

The memorization and recitation of their literary heritage has always been vital to Iranians, whose attitude toward the power of the written and spoken word is reverential. Even today the national passion for poetry is constantly expressed over radio and television, in teahouses, in literary societies, in daily conversation, and in the Musha'areh, the poetry recitation contest. Nizami's work serves as a vehicle and a symbol of this tradition, for it unites universality with deep-rooted artistic endeavor, a sense of justice and passion for the arts and sciences with spirituality and genuine piety. For richness and fineness of metaphor, accuracy, and profundity of psychological observation, and sheer virtuosity of storytelling, Nizami is unequaled.

1. *Khamseh* means quintet. The five long epic poems of Nizami are also known collectively as the *Panj-Ganj*, or *Five Treasures*. They contain approximately thirty thousand distichs or about sixty thousand lines.

2. A *masnavi* is a string of distichs rhyming in pairs, used mainly for long epic poems of a heroic, historic, and romantic character, as well as for didactic, philosophical, and mystical poems.

3. With few exceptions, notably Gurgani, the *masnavi* was used mainly for heroic epics by the poets who preceded Nizami. An important contribution of the Persians to world literature is the mystical and lyric

ghazal, a kind of sonnet used for lyric love verses and for verses expressing life's mysteries, joys, and sorrows. Another poetical form popular with the Persians and used especially in their panegyric court poetry is the *qasideh,* an ode or elegy. The *ruba'i,* or quatrain, is still another popular verse form used by almost all Persian poets, and is familiar to Western readers through Edward Fitzgerald's translation of the work of Omar Khayyam.

4. This manuscript was completed in 763 A.H./May 1362 A.D., and is to be found in the Bibliothèque Nationale, Paris. See E. Blochet, *Catalogue des manuscrits persans de la Bibliothèque Nationale,* vol. 3, no. 1247. Other famous manuscripts from the fourteenth century (completed in 766 A.H./January 1365 A.D.) are found in the Bodleian Library, Oxford, England. See Sachau-Ethé, *Catalogue of the Persian, Turkish, Hindustani, and Pushtu manuscripts in the Bodleian Library,* Oxford, 1889, no. 585. For another Bibliothèque Nationale, Paris, manuscript completed in 767 A.H./August 1366 A.D., see Suppl. Persan 580. There are several famous manuscripts in the museums and libraries of the Soviet Union. The oldest is the manuscript, completed in 1375 A.D., found in the Library of Leningrad University, registered under the number MS0354.

5. Nizami is the pen name of Hakim Jamal al-din Abu Muhammad Ilyas ibn Yusuf ibn Zaki Mu'ayyad. Persian poets have long devised pen names from the names of patrons, from personal characteristics, or from other significant circumstances, and have made an art of weaving them into their poems. One purpose of the pen name, or *takhallus,* was to safeguard against plagiarism, but it was often not effective.

6. Some of Nizami's biographers speak of him as Nizami of Qum rather than Nizami of Ganjeh.

7. Edward G. Browne, *A Literary History of Persia,* vol. 2 (London, 1906), p. 403.

8. Henry Blochmann, *The Prosody of the Persians According to Saifi, Jami, and Other Writers* (Amsterdam, 1970), p. 1.

9. Nizami of Ganja, *The Haft Paikar* ("The Seven Beauties"), translated from the Persian with a commentary by C. E. Wilson (London, 1924), p. XVI.

10. A. J. Arberry, *The Legacy of Persia* (Oxford, 1968), p. 213.

THE KHAMSEH OF 1524/25

The manuscript copy of Nizami's *Khamseh,* which is now in the collection of the Islamic Department of the Metropolitan Museum, is a splendid example of the high level of bookmaking achieved in early sixteenth-century Iran. The calligraphy, illumination, even the paper and binding, express the Persian people's reverence and delight for books and the unity and perfection of design which their artisans sought.

The Museum's manuscript measures 12¾ × 8¾ inches. Although most of the gilding has worn off the tooled leather binding, the pictured landscape—with grazing deer and birds in flight—is appealing to both the eye and the touch. The binding envelops the book, carefully protecting the highly polished, gold-flecked pages inside.

The reverse side of the binding is embellished with a complex geometric design which is reproduced on the cover of this volume. The technique used to execute this design, which was developed during the fifteenth century to answer the demand for ever more elaborately decorative bindings, ingeniously combines leather with paper. This technique is most easily appreciated in the large center medallion. Gold-tooled maroon leather was cut to frame the central and corner medallions; then a layer of bright blue paper was placed within the cut-out spaces to provide a strongly contrasting background for the overlay of fine arabesque scrolls and interlocking lobed medallions which were cut from a single thickness of light brown leather. Finally, certain areas were gilded to create a pattern in two levels. The same technique of paper and leather montage is also used in the binding's outer frame. In it large medallions with delicate arabesque scrolls and flowing calligraphy are contrasted with smaller units having tightly organized arabesques. The two colorful sections of the bindings are separated by a gilded and tooled frame which forms a rich contrast to the colors of the other areas.

Although the circles and ellipses were produced with the aid of a compass, subtle variations in the shape of the edges of the medallions and the complex relationship of the many elements of the design prevent monotony. The patterns are carefully organized, but the intricacy of the whole discourages mathematical analysis. Instead, the eye is led from curve to countercurve, and the circles appear magically interwoven with one another, inspiring contemplative viewing.

Because bookmaking in the Islamic world centered on the copying of the Koran, calligraphy developed as an act of piety as well as an art form. The educated appreciated the physical beauty of calligraphy; connoisseurs prided themselves on their ability to identify the writing of well-known calligraphers, and collectors paid large sums of money for their work. It became customary for rulers to employ famous calligraphers to copy their official correspondences and royal decrees.

The colophon of the Metropolitan Museum's *Khamseh* states that the calligrapher was Sultan Muhammad ibn Nur Allah. Sultan Muhammad Nur was born about 1472 in Herat, a major cultural center in northeastern Iran, and studied with Sultan Ali Mashhadi, the leading calligrapher of the court of Husayn Bayqara, the last Timurid ruler of Persia. He specialized in a fine and graceful script, known as *Khafi,* which can be seen in the opening lines of the *Khamseh* (opposite) and in several of the illustrations in which text and picture are combined (miniatures 1, 3, 5, and 9). Sultan Muhammad Nur may have been the illuminator of this manuscript, as in the colophons of other works he calls himself *modhahheb,* or illuminator.

The basic element of the decoration is an arabesque scroll embellished with multicolored blossoms and set against a blue, gold, or black background. The horizontal rectangular panels, divided into smaller units by interlocking lobed medallions, offsets the narrow panels of the text; the whole is given added unity by the striking black background of the larger rectangular frame. While this type of geometric design is ultimately a descendant of the decoration found on early Koranic manuscripts, the complex patterns in this manuscript are characteristic of the illuminators of the early sixteenth century.

Each of the three stories translated here is headed by similarly illuminated panels using the same components but in differing arrangements. The ornamentation at the beginning of "The Seven Princesses" (miniature 6) bears a strong resemblance to the geometric designs used on the inner binding. This suggests that the binding may have been designed by the illuminator to be copied by the leather workers. At the time this manuscript was made, luxurious books were often produced in ateliers where calligraphers, illuminators, binders, and painters worked together; therefore such cooperation would not have been unusual.

Although the traditions of bookmaking and illumination were well developed by the tenth century, the illustration of manuscripts was not common in Persia until the early thirteenth century. The Mongol invasions of the Near East during the thirteenth century caused only a brief disruption in the progress of miniature

An inside cover of the *Khamseh* of 1524/25

painting; the Mongol rulers and high government officials were extremely interested in the documentation of their history and commissioned many fine manuscripts, some of which were illustrated with elaborate scenes of battlefields and ceremonies. The Mongol state disintegrated in the middle of the fourteenth century, but bookmaking continued to flourish under their successors. The production of fine manuscripts combining the arts of calligraphy, illumination, painting, and binding was given great impetus by patronage of members of the Timurid dynasty. While the financing of the construction of mosques and other religious institutions showed a patron's concern for public welfare, the manuscripts he commissioned reflected his private tastes. Manuscripts were also prepared as gifts.

The most important of the artisans of the late Timurid period were the calligrapher Sultan Ali Mashhadi and the painter Behzad, who worked in Herat during the reign of Husayn Bayqara (1468–1506). A copy of the *Bustan* of Sa'di, dated 1488, is signed by both of them and provides an example of the high level of their joint achievement. Behzad's paintings exhibit two clear characteristics: human figures are presented in a natural lifelike manner and are differentiated by posture and gesture with less concern for the detail of their costumes, while every pattern of the tile work, inlaid woodwork, and wickerwork of the buildings is meticulously rendered. Behzad balances the realism of individual figures with the formalism of palaces and pavilions by careful distribution of groups of figures within the spaces created by the architectural setting. These groupings often reflect the highly developed sense of protocol which characterized the Timurid dynasty. The dialogue between realism and formalism became a mark of the Herat style; some painters preferred to emphasize movement and space while others concentrated on the meticulous rendering of details.

The identity of the illustrator of the Metropolitan Museum's *Khamseh* is not certain, but the miniatures in the manuscript clearly follow the Herat tradition. Although some of the pictures are closely related to an episode in the text, others seem more intent on depicting the life and customs and perhaps even the personalities of the Safavid court of the time. The colophon establishes this as 931 A.H. or between October 1524 and October 1525; one of the paintings is dated Rajab 931 or April/May 1525 (miniature 4).

The dimensions of an illustration were usually determined by the space which the calligrapher left for it when copying the text. In this manuscript most of the miniatures occupy an entire page, but sometimes the painter has had to incorporate sections of the text within his paintings. In many cases, the integration is successful as in "The Black Pavilion" (miniature 6). In others, however, it disturbs the composition; in "The Red Pavilion" (miniature 9) the painter was forced to place the dome of the pavilion in the margin of the page.

The perspective follows the conventions of Persian painting by showing each object from the point of view necessary to make it comprehensible. Thus pools are shown from above, and different angles of vision are used to articulate the relationship of various sections of buildings. For example, in "The Sandalwood Pavilion" (miniature 11), the columns, the flat roof, and the polygonal cap-dome in the middle of the roof are each seen from different perspectives.

The illustrator also follows the conventions of this period in his use of color. The posture of a figure is indicated by the use of outline and further emphasized by strong color contrasts between the various levels of clothing, as well as between the figure and the background. The effectiveness of this method of indicating volume, however, is often counteracted by this painter's love of detail, which sometimes caused him to cover garments with small-scale patterns. A comparison of the figures of Bahram Gur in the red and the white pavilions makes this clear (miniatures 9 and 12).

Among the most delightful of the miniatures in the Metropolitan Museum's *Khamseh* are those illustrating the story of "Khrosow and Shirin." The series opens with Khosrow's discovery of Shirin bathing in a wilderness pool (miniature 1). It is the climax of the first section of the romance, a moment long favored by Nizami illustrators. The lovers meet without recognizing each other, yet each suspects the other is the beloved. The landscape is divided diagonally; the upper part is warm, sunlit, and barren, dominated by the proportionately large figure of Khosrow; the lower is cool, dark, and intimate. By careful modulation of colors, attention is drawn from the partly naked Shirin, sitting in the shimmering silver water (it has oxidized to dark gray) with flowers and ducks nearby, to the brilliantly clad and superbly mounted Khosrow, whose figure is outlined by a golden sky. Although the composition is simple, the painting captures the spirit of the poetry. Nizami describes Shirin as a moon surrounded by the dark night sky and, in the painting, the luminosity of her body contrasts beautifully with the darkness of her hair and the cloth she has wrapped around the lower part of her body. But the painting departs in one crucial respect from the episode as it is related in the text. According to Nizami, Shirin is supposed to recognize Khosrow by his scarlet garments, and it is because he has changed them to escape his enemies that she does not know who he is. The illustrator obviously has chosen to ignore this important fact, probably in order to achieve a more colorful and balanced composition.

The second picture of the series is of Khosrow's reinstatement on Iran's throne after he had driven away his rival, Bahram Chubin. The event, of great significance in the life of the historic Khosrow Parviz, is barely mentioned by Nizami, who was more interested in Khosrow's longing for Shirin than in his military triumph. The ruler is seated on a throne with, as was traditional, a luxurious carpet beneath his feet and a canopy above his head. He is surrounded by his court: a gray-headed man is kneeling before him, having probably just kissed the carpet in obeisance; on the left are attendants bearing his weapons and drinking cup; and to the right is a youth, perhaps his own son.

The focus of the painting, however, is in the foreground, where a group of men are gathered. There are *yasauls* with knobbed sticks who were responsible for keeping order at public audiences, a gold-turbaned man with a sword suggesting he is a high military official, and a beautiful youth in a brocaded cloak standing beside a sad white-bearded man who, in contrast to the other men, has a brownish complexion. The range of physical types and attitudes is wide, and the painter has depicted them with great care.

The pair of figures just below the carpet on the right is particularly noteworthy. The bearded man wearing a long blue coat appears to be reading from a piece of paper which he holds in his hand, while a youth places ink on the seal-ring he wears on his little finger. The older man seems ready to stamp the paper from which he reads and could indeed be the keeper of the royal seal, a lucrative and respected position in the Safavid administration. The younger man with the pen and ink case tucked in his belt is probably his assistant.

More than an illustration for Nizami's poem, this miniature is a diagram of the contemporary Safavid court. It is possible that most of the persons attending the ruler are portraits of officials known to the artist. Some scholars have suggested that Khosrow was intended to represent the Safavid ruler Shah Isma'il. That, however, is unlikely, as Isma'il had been dead for more than a year when this manuscript was completed; nor could it have been a likeness of his son and successor, as he was only eleven years old at that time. It is more probable the person portrayed as Khosrow was the governor of Herat, Durmish Khan Shamlu. Although it cannot be proved with certainty, it is possible that the patron of the manuscript was the keeper of the seal and that he commissioned it as a gift to Durmish Khan Shamlu.

The painting depicting Shirin's visit to the stoneworker Farhad (miniature 3) has the simplicity of the wilderness bathing scene but none of its passion or intimacy. The milk canal which Farhad has built to please and win Shirin forms a barrier between them. Farhad, dressed in simple clothes, is surrounded by the tools of his trade—axes, a chisel, a spade, and a water gourd—while Shirin is richly garbed; she is wearing a golden coronet and is accompanied by two watchful ladies-in-waiting. Although carefully painted, the scene does not express the emotional intensity of Nizami's poetry. Curiously, one of the most interesting sections of the painting is the rock outcropping in the upper left on which stand two partridges and a gazelle. The edges of the rocks as well as those near Shirin's attendants, suggest the profiles of animal and human heads.

The illustrator returns to the theme of courtly splendor in his painting of the wedding of Khosrow and Shirin (miniature 4). The design is stately and at the same time intimate. The artist has lavished particular attention on the portico of the place in which the lovers are seated. Although no such buildings survive in Herat today, similar porticos, constructed between the sixteenth and the nineteenth centuries are to be found on buildings in Bokhara. It is likely, therefore, that the artist intended to depict a specific building and that he was endeavoring to flatter its owner by comparing him to Khosrow Parviz. There is sufficient individuality in the face of Khosrow to suggest that it is a portrait of a known person. The inscription on the portico, praising the beauty of the building as "soul-refreshing" and "attractive," also bears the date Rajab 931, which further suggests that this painting commemorates the construction of a particular building and that the man depicted as Khosrow was its owner.

Architectural ornamentation is also a major component of the miniature of Layla and Majnun at school (miniature 5). Neither Nizami nor the artist were faithful to the fact that Layla and Majnun lived in Arabia; both preferred to introduce more familiar contemporary Iranian scenes. The building represented is a *madraseh*, a typical medieval Persian religious educational institution. The classroom is a small mosque and is fronted by an open courtyard surrounded by rooms in which the students and teachers lived. The *madraseh*, built by Husayn Bayqara during his reign in Herat, for instance, was said to have housed ten thousand students—probably a conventional figure meaning a large number. One, endowed by the poet-statesman Ali Shir Neva'i, served as a home for the poet Jami. Such schools would have been familiar to both the painter and the calligrapher of this manuscript; they may well have received their basic instruction in one of them.

That the setting is a mosque is indicated by the *muezzin* standing on the corner of the roof of the building. His hands are raised to amplify his voice as he recites the call to prayer; his posture and expression show he is straining to make his voice as loud as possible.

Below, the composition of the classroom and courtyard is arranged around a series of vignettes: a small boy is chasing a companion, rock in hand; a student naps as another rubs his paper against a special board in order to impress it with guidelines for writing; several students are memorizing letters written on their tablets or text from the books they hold in their hands; and one kneels before the teacher with evident concern for the staff in his right hand. The figure of the white-bearded master, his tattered cloak hanging carelessly from his slightly humped back, shows the artist's skill at characterization. His interest in depicting useful tools, as in the painting of Shirin and Farhad, is evidenced by his careful placement of the ink and brush holders and the bookstands and water jugs.

While the groups of students are painted in a lively way, their activities do not serve to illustrate Nizami's text; the meeting of Layla and Majnun is, in fact, merely used as a pretext for a genre painting. It is even difficult to decide which of the students are Layla and Majnun. They are probably the girl in brown and blue and the boy in blue seated opposite each other on the Persian carpet, for there is gold embroidery on her cloak and she wears the golden headdress typical of court attendants. Although Nizami stresses that Layla and Majnun were so absorbed in each other that they were unable to concentrate on their work, the painter has shown them performing the same tasks as the other students. The inscription exhorts the teacher to treat Layla justly, since beauty deserves goodness. This theme is not found in Nizami's text and appears rather to be a commentary on the painting itself.

A similar love of complex ornaments and devotion to setting rather than story is seen in the miniatures illustrating "The Seven Princesses." Bahram Gur's meetings with each of the princesses are presented as courtly entertainments basically similar in composition though differing in detail. In each, Bahram and the princess are seated apart from each other and are accompanied by musicians or other attendants who often ignore the royal pair. Sometimes glimpses of a garden appear at the edges of the painting, suggesting buildings set in a large enclosure, like the garden residences built in Herat by the Timurids and used also by the Safavid governors and their royal wards (miniatures 7 and 8). In other paintings, the room where Bahram and the princess sit overlooks a courtyard containing a fountain (miniatures 6 and 11).

Internal evidence indicates that these miniatures were executed in two stages: first the architectural setting with Bahram and the princess was fully drawn and painted; then the court attendants were added to balance the composition. This can be seen in the paintings of the black and the white pavilions, which have been slightly damaged. In the black pavilion (miniature 6), the tile patterns continue under the candles; and in the white pavilion (miniature 12), a water-stain has removed portions of two attendants on the left, revealing the unbroken pattern of the courtyard tiles.

This two-step process is reflected also in the manner in which the figures are presented. Bahram Gur and the princesses are often stiffly posed, while the attitudes of their attendants seem more natural and spontaneous. In the turquoise pavilion, for example, the musicians converse as they play and a third woman reads a manuscript. In the sandalwood pavilion, three attendants play blindman's bluff, apparently oblivious to the stately tableau behind them (miniatures 10 and 11).

The artist has used various methods to unify these separate segments. A favorite device involves the use of color to create an equilateral triangle which, with Bahram as its apex, links the two groups of figures (miniatures 7 and 9). Sometimes the princess is placed at the apex of a second triangular grouping (miniature 10). However, this color system made it difficult for the painter to be faithful to Nizami's text, which dictates that all persons present in each pavilion wear clothing of the color associated with its governing heavenly body. This departure from the text is most noticeable in the paintings of the green and red pavilions (miniatures 8 and 9).

Although Bahram Gur appears to be the focal point of most of these paintings, the inscriptions on the buildings refer to the princesses and to their pavilions. For example, the turquoise pavilion is said to reach to the sky and the whiteness of the white pavilion is compared to eyes purified by tears. This miniature contains a second symbol of tears; in the foreground is a clump of narcissus. In poetry, the eyes of a lover red with weeping for the absent beloved is often compared to that flower.

The painting of the yellow pavilion has two unusual features. The building's inscription does not refer to the scene represented, but to the originator of the form of script used in the painting. It says: "I have heard that on this golden pavilion, there is a script which ultimately belongs to Mahmud." The implication is that whoever wrote it used a script invented by someone named Mahmud. This was common practice, for student calligraphers often claimed that they used a script invented by their teachers. In his biographical dictionary, Ali Shir Neva'i mentions a calligrapher named Mahmud Harawi who, it seems, taught other calligraphers in the generation of Sultan Muhammad Nur. This enigmatic inscription suggests that perhaps he too was a student of Mahmud Harawi.

The second unusual feature in the painting of the yellow pavilion is that the attendant who carries a cup and a flask bears so strong a resemblance to the portrait of Khosrow in the marriage miniature that it may have been intended to represent and flatter the same important personnage.

Although they are somewhat stiff and repetitive, the miniatures illustrating "The Seven Princesses" exert a special fascination. The subtle variations on a single theme have an elegance which reflects the courtly setting in which Nizami's poetry was read and appreciated. The artist also employs both of the major elements that characterize Herat painting. His interest in realism is evident in the casual groupings of court attendants, while his balanced use of color and of elaborate architectural patterns express Herat's formal tradition.

Some of the paintings of the Metropolitan Museum's *Khamseh* reflect the tone and substance of Nizami's poetry, while others relate more closely to the time and place in which they were created. They provide a link between the style of painting popular in fifteenth-century Herat and that used by sixteenth-century painters working for the Safavids.

The *Khamseh* as a whole is a splendid example of the art of the Persian book in general and in particular reflects the high level of this art achieved under the patronage of the royal family and high court officials in the ateliers of Herat in early sixteenth-century Persia.

PRISCILLA P. SOUCEK
Department of the History of Art
University of Michigan

Khosrow and Shirin

In the land of Persia, long ago, lived King Hormuzd the Great. Called "the light of the world's justice," he was the son of the illustrious Khosrow Anushirvan, who had been a king of great renown in his own time. For many years King Hormuzd awaited an heir, a son to assure the continuation of his line. Night and day he prayed to God, and when at last a son was born, his gratitude was boundless. And as his son grew, so grew the king's thankfulness, for the child was a bounding boy of winning eloquence.

Named Khosrow for his grandfather, the boy was called Parviz, "the Victorious One"—such was the king's delight in him. The crown prince excelled in all he did. No star in the northern sky shone with greater brilliance than this magnitude-to-be. By the age of nine he was schooled in all the learned disciplines; in five years more he was an expert horseman and accomplished hunter. A wizard with the sword, the spear, and the arrow, Khosrow soon mastered the art of war. His skill would one day make his beloved Persia the glittering mistress of the East.

Now in the court of Hormuzd was a sage, Bozorg Omid by name, who took it upon himself to counsel both father and son. As he admitted Khosrow to the mysteries of the stars and the even more subtle ways of man and beast, he entreated Hormuzd to be a just and worthy ruler. "What use, Magnificence, to guard your own good with zeal while the state of your subjects goes untended? Who will grant a throne respect when those who uphold it have nothing? The rights of the ruled must always rule: let this byword never leave your thoughts."

Hormuzd, wise son of a wise father, accepted this advice and proclaimed new laws to a fanfare of trumpets. Hormuzd promised to protect his people against theft and destruction of property and to guard the privacy of their homes. Stern edicts, respecting no one person more than another, assured redress for all. And of all the youths in Persia, none admired the uprightness of the king more than his own son.

One morning, he who was the court's darling rode forth to the hunt. Little did Khosrow know, as the sun rose and climbed to the top of its blue dome, that his father's clarion commands would ring so close to his own ears.

It was a glorious day. The sun was bright; the air was clear; and best of all, the game was plentiful. Then, as the sun began its descent, Khosrow and his companions came upon a pleasant settlement on the green plain. The young prince commandeered a peasant's house for food and lodging, and soon the revelry began. Inspired by his minstrel's tunes and the abundant wine, Khosrow and his companions rocked the house with cheers and drank throughout the night. Lost in wine and laughter, Khosrow was unaware that one of his servants had reeled into the vineyard to pick grapes and so frightened the prince's horse that the steed reared, broke loose, and trampled the peasant's newly sprouted crops.

Daybreak saw the bleary-eyed huntsmen home. With the rising of the golden sun, the outraged peasant's complaint reached the court. Khosrow was brought before the king at once. "No sooner do my decrees go forth than they are trampled by your horse's hooves! Since when, my high-born son, are you to take pleasure at my people's cost?"

The penalties were harsh. The man who had picked the grapes was given to the owner of the vineyard as a slave; the hooves of Khosrow's horse were ruthlessly cut; and Khosrow's princely throne was given to the peasant. Then the minstrel's fingernails were clipped and his harp was unstrung.

Ashamed that his companions should be punished for his sake and pained by his father's wrath, Khosrow begged the elders of the court to plead for his pardon. The counselors, who dearly loved the prince, went to Hormuzd with an apology. So strong was his regret that Khosrow dressed himself in a shroud, took a sharp sword, wept bitterly and writhed on the ground. "Here is my sword, and my submissive head. I can bear any sorrow of this life but the anger of the king." When Hormuzd heard of this speech, he kissed Khosrow and forgave him and made him once again crown prince.

That night, in a dream, Khosrow was visited by his grandfather, Khosrow Anushirvan. "Listen to me," said the old man, "I foresee your happy future because of your willingness to accept chastisement. In place of what you have lost, you will receive four things of even greater worth: you shall ride Shabdiz, the world's swiftest and most fabled steed, who will shake his mane to your glory across a mighty empire bordered by the seas; you shall sit on Taqdis, the throne of thrones, which makes your throne surrendered but a bench; at your bidding Barbad the musician shall play and with the lightest touch will far surpass the broken notes of your lost minstrel. But beyond all these, you shall have Shirin, your destined love, whose sweetness and beauty will sustain you all your days." With this last promise, Khosrow Anushirvan vanished, and the prince awoke.

Now Khosrow's dearest friend and second self was the youth Shapur, a painter of great skill and self-confidence. "When I draw a person's head, it moves; the bird whose wing I draw will fly," he was wont to boast. It was said of Shapur that his art was so magical that he could draw pictures on water. At portraiture Shapur excelled; he could capture not only the likeness but the subject's very soul.

A born adventurer, Shapur had traveled far and wide. One day, while recounting to Khosrow the many marvels he had seen, Shapur told of a journey to Armenia. He praised the beauty of the mountains, the splendor of the court, and the Armenian queen Mihin Banu. A woman of great wealth and property, Mihin Banu had no husband, yet passed her life content and was stronger than any man. But above all he praised the queen's niece, Shirin. "Her face is a wild rose, and her lips are as sweet as her name. Her charming words please everyone, and she has been chosen as the heir of Queen Mihin Banu. Never have I seen a maiden as enchanting as Shirin! And never have I seen anything like the queen's black horse Shabdiz!"

"Shirin! Did you say Shirin? How astonishing! How fortunate!" Then Khosrow told his friend about the dream and sent Shapur at once to bring Shirin to him. "If she be like wax, impress her with our seal. If her heart be iron, return at once and tell me so that I shall not strike cold iron!"

Thus was Shapur instructed; he promised not to fail. "Fear not, my prince! As long as my brushes and paints attend me, failure has no chance!" And so he departed.

When he reached Armenia it was spring; the mountains were covered with flowers, and the woods and fields were green. While riding, Shapur came upon an aged priest, who lived in a small, ancient monastery carved out of rock high up on a cliff. The old man told a curious tale. "At the foot of this very mountain is a cave, and in the cave is a black stone that every horseman in the world would covet—if he only knew of it. From nearby and faraway plains the swift mares come to this great stone and, when in heat, rub themselves against it. Every foal born to these mares is wonderfully swift; but the swiftest of all is Shabdiz, that horse of lightning hooves, the stallion of our queen."

"I know of him," Shapur replied, and told the priest that he had traveled to Armenia to visit the court. Then the old man pointed to a pretty meadow where the royal party was accustomed to spreading their picnic cloth.

The next morning, at dawn, Shapur went to the pretty meadow. He took a piece of paper in his hand and sketched a portrait of the prince, a likeness so exact as to make the most reluctant maiden swoon. Then he hung the picture from a branch of a tree and hid himself. He did not have to wait long, for soon Shirin appeared with her attendants.

The day shimmered with promise; every leaf danced in the breeze. Shirin and her companions spread their carpets on the grass, and, sipping wine, amused themselves with singing, dancing to the music of lutes, and fashioning wreathes of flowers for each other. Then, at last, Shirin noticed the portrait. She asked that it be brought to her. She held it in her hands and gazed at the handsome prince. Then her heart dissolved with joy and she embraced the portrait. Frightened at her trembling, and supposing that the picture was the work of evil spirits, her handmaidens destroyed the image and burned rue to stop the spell. Only then did Shirin recover her senses, and the party moved on.

The following morning, Shapur again went to the meadow, made a portrait of the prince, hung it from a branch, and hid. When Shirin appeared and saw the portrait, her soul again took flight. But this time her maids refused to bring the picture to her. They rolled up their carpets and the party fled.

On the third morning, Shirin and her companions set out for a different meadow. Following them, Shapur made yet another portrait, hung it as before, and hid himself. Soon Shirin caught sight of it. She seized it from the branch herself and worshipped it as if it were an idol. In its homage she drank wine; with every sip she kissed the ground. At last, she sent her maids to search for someone who might be able to explain the mystery; but not a soul could be found. Then, at the far end of the meadow, Shirin noticed a stranger. Believing that this person had some knowledge of the portrait, she instructed her attendants to ask if he knew the name and rank of the one who had captured her heart.

When Shapur—for the stranger was none other than the painter—saw the maidens approach, he knew that his stratagem had not failed. To their inquiries, he answered that the secret could be imparted only to Shirin herself. When the maidens gave this message to their mistress, Shirin ran eagerly across the field. As she drew near, Shapur was overwhelmed, so delicate was her beauty.

"Who might you be? Where are you from? What do you know?" she breathlessly asked. Shapur replied that he had traveled far and wide, that he could unlock many mysteries and would divulge the story of the portrait, but only if they were left entirely alone. Shirin dismissed her maidens. The painter then told her that the one she loved was a fine prince, Khosrow Parviz by name. She then confessed that her happiness was so entwined with the portrait that she worshipped it night and day. Whereupon Shapur told how the prince had dreamed about Shirin, his destined love, and had sent him to Armenia to find her. As Shapur spoke, Shirin was overcome with joy.

Then the painter, ever ingenious, devised a plan. The next morning, at dawn, Shirin was to ride to the hunt on Shabdiz and flee from her companions—so swift was the steed that she would not be caught—and she was to journey toward Persia. Then Shapur gave Shirin a seal ring belonging to Khosrow and told her to show it to anyone she met along the way. Perhaps the stranger she met would be Khosrow himself. Shirin would recognize him, for he would be garbed in red from head to foot; his horse's hooves would be shod with gold. Should Shirin not encounter Khosrow, she must go to the royal palace Moshku, in the capital city of Mada'in, and show the seal ring to the servants there.

Then, with great pride and pleasure in the powers of his palette, Shapur departed; the princess summoned her attendants and returned to the palace of Queen Mihin Banu. That night she pleaded with the queen to be allowed to ride on Shabdiz the next day. As the stallion was exceedingly strong-spirited, the queen was reluctant to agree, but agree she did.

At dawn, Shirin and her attendants made ready for the hunt. Dressed in a manly manner, as was the custom in Armenia for hunting on the plains, the party rode forth at a gallop. Soon Shabdiz had left the other horses far behind. Shirin's companions tried to follow, but in vain, and after spending the day in fruitless search they rode back to the palace with their doleful news. Throughout the night the good queen wept and mourned, but then she had a dream: her beloved falcon flew away, and as she grieved it returned. She took this as a happy omen, and so the next morning, to the amazement of her court, no search was called.

Meanwhile, Shirin rode toward Persia in search of her beloved prince. For fourteen days and fourteen nights she traveled. Then she came upon an emerald field in which there gleamed a gentle pool. Weary and covered with dust from head to foot, she stopped. When she had satisfied herself that she was quite alone, she tethered Shabdiz and prepared to bathe. Beautiful was the whiteness of her skin against the blueness of the water. She loosed her braids and washed her long black hair, and the moon-like reflection of her face was caught in the shallows of the pool. And then she sat in the cool, refreshing water, dreaming of Khosrow.

She did not know that from the very day Khosrow had sent Shapur to Armenia, fate had sent ill fortune to the prince. For Khosrow had enemies in Persia; men who had envied him from the hour of his birth. Now they began to strike coins in his name and to circulate them in the cities of the realm. Hormuzd, thinking his son was plotting to seize the throne, ordered the prince cast into prison. When the good sage Bozorg Omid heard of the decree, he urged Khosrow to flee.

Khosrow rode directly to the palace and told his servants that he would be hunting for a fortnight. If, meanwhile, a beauty appeared, riding a black stallion like a peacock on a raven's back, she was to be welcomed as an honored guest and given every courtesy. Indeed, if the palace was not to her liking, another was to be built for her in any place she might prefer. "See to this as you would to your own safety!" Khosrow ordered and then, disguising himself in robes other than his customary red, he departed for Armenia. So swiftly did he ride

that he covered two days' distance in one. Then, stopping, he ordered his attendants to feed their horses while he rode on alone. Suddenly, he came upon the pool in the emerald field and saw Shirin sitting in the water like a lily. At the sight of her his heart caught fire and burned; he trembled with desire in every limb. Softly he rode toward her and whispered to himself how he would like to have such a beautiful maiden and such a black horse as hers, little knowing that one day they would both be his.

Suddenly Shirin looked up. Startled, she gathered her black hair about her like a cloak, emerged from the pool, dressed, and mounted her horse. At the touch of her heel Shabdiz carried her off into the shadows of the late afternoon. Watching her, Khosrow was as much astonished by the swiftness of her flight as by her beauty. When she had disappeared he wept, then continued his journey toward Armenia.

As she rode, Shirin dwelled on the stranger from whom she had fled. She wondered if he might have been Khosrow even though he was not garbed in red, as Shapur had advised.

Riding on, Shirin finally reached the palace Moshku. She presented the prince's ring and was welcomed with great ceremony; Shabdiz was taken to the stable. When she was asked to tell her story, she refused; she would wait until Khosrow's return. Weeks went by like flights of swallows with not a word from Khosrow. Shirin became uneasy; the palace did not please her, as no window offered happy views. She longed for the green mountains of Armenia; at last she became so restive that the maidservants told her of Khosrow's command that a new residence be built for her should she desire. Shirin eagerly requested that a new palace be built on a mountain plain. The servants, envying her beauty and her privilege, arranged, instead, for the palace to be built in an unhealthy place; a place so hot, the saying went, that it could make a child into an old man in less than a week. It was a place not far from Kermanshah, but far, indeed, from the world. To this prison-palace did Shirin repair, where grief was her constant companion.

By this time, Khosrow had reached the borders of Armenia. When Queen Mihin Banu heard of his arrival, she went with all her retinue to welcome him. A chair was placed for him at the foot of her throne, and she commanded that great festivities be held in his honor. Musicians played, girls danced, and in every tent a fire burned and lavish feasts were set. Game, fruits, and wine were as abundant as the pasturelands and orchards of Armenia. But for Khosrow the wine was bitter; even as he dallied with the pretty maidens, he drank only his desire for Shirin.

One night in the midst of these amusements, Shapur appeared at Khosrow's tent. He kissed the ground before the prince and told of what had passed: how he had

MINIATURE I   *Khosrow discovers Shirin bathing in a wilderness pool*

found Shirin and had worked magic with his paints and how Shirin had ridden off on Shabdiz—surely she was at the palace Moshku even now—and he greatly praised her beauty and strong-mindedness. So overjoyed was Khosrow when he heard these words that he covered his friend with jewels and gave him a precious robe. Then he ordered Shapur to go to Shirin as quickly as a moth flies toward a light.

Soon afterward Queen Mihin Banu happened to come to Khosrow's tent, and the prince told her of the messenger who had brought news of Shirin; the faithful Shapur would be sent to bring her back from Persia. As he made ready to depart, the queen ordered her second-swiftest steed, Golgun—sired, like Shabdiz, in the mountain cave—given to Shapur to take with him in case Shirin no longer had Shabdiz. Within the hour, Shapur set out, mounted on his own horse and leading the splendid Golgun.

At last he arrived in Persia and found the disconsolate princess sequestered in her wretched palace. Upon seeing Shapur, Shirin trembled with joy, so long had she despaired of word from Khosrow. The next morning, at the golden break of dawn, they departed in haste for Armenia; Shirin rode Golgun, for Shabdiz had remained in the stable at the palace Moshku. When they reached the court of Queen Mihin Banu there was rejoicing beyond imagining, so happy was the queen to see Shirin.

But while Shapur and Shirin were on their way to Armenia, word had come to Khosrow of the death of his father King Hormuzd, and he had hurried back to Persia to claim his rightful throne. He arrived in the capital city of Mada'in hoping to find Shirin, but she had already departed. Her black stallion Shabdiz was still in the stable, and so to console himself in her absence, Khosrow rode Shabdiz to the hunt, for the young king greatly enjoyed that sport. And after the hunt, he took his pleasure in drinking fine wine.

Khosrow ruled with justice, like his father and grandfather before him, and his subjects were well pleased. But their contentment had not long to last, for soon Bahram Chubin, the wily general who had commanded the armies under Hormuzd, devised a treacherous scheme to seize the throne. He had it whispered among the people that Khosrow had ordered his father killed, and that he was a murderer and unfit to wear the Persian crown. He also had it whispered that Khosrow valued a gulp of wine more than the blood of a hundred brothers, that he would surrender his kingdom for a price, and that he was so distracted by his love for Shirin that he could not rule. Thus did the evil Bahram Chubin spread his subtle plague and turn the people against Khosrow, and once again Khosrow was forced to flee his native land. Under cover of night he saddled Shabdiz and rode toward Armenia—and Shirin. He traveled on without a rest until he neared

Detail from MINIATURE I

the capital of Armenia. Here he interrupted his wearisome journey for the diversion of a hunt.

Now it happened that Shirin also rode to the hunt that morning. And, as was her custom, she rode far ahead of her attendants, for she was ever more spirited than they. In a clearing she came upon a stranger, the very one who had surprised her while she was bathing in the wilderness pool. It was, indeed, Khosrow. A thousand times more beautiful than Khosrow had remembered, was Shirin. Dazzling was the sun at the moment of their encounter, but even more dazzling were their eyes. They reined in their horses and sat gazing at one another, not daring to move lest the slightest motion break the spell. When at last they had regained their senses, Khosrow dismounted and extended his hand; Shirin slipped from her horse with the grace of a dancer. For a moment they spoke. Khosrow told of his troubles, and Shirin invited him to the palace. Then her attendants found her; she ordered them to hasten to the queen with the happy news.

When Queen Mihin Banu learned of Khosrow's return, she was beside herself with joy. She prepared gifts worthy of a king and arranged for feasts and celebrations. She went forth herself to welcome him to the palace and scattered his path with jewels. But the most precious gift she had to offer was the princess Shirin. Though she could see how intensely Khosrow loved Shirin and how Shirin loved Khosrow, the good queen drew her niece aside and warned her that although Khosrow ruled with justice, she must guard herself against deceit. She must not satisfy all his desires lest he tire of her, for it was said that in the land of Persia he possessed a thousand beauties. "Keep your jewel, and he will be as addicted to you as to opium. Yield, and you will be a trampled flower before the world. If he is the moon, you are the sun," she counseled. And Shirin swore, by the seven heavens, that even if she wept tears of blood for love of Khosrow, she would not be his until she was his wife. And so the queen allowed Shirin to sit by Khosrow's side in the festivities, but forbade them to converse privately or be left to themselves.

How perfect for the lovers were these ecstatic days! The air sparkled; the sky was never so blue, the grass so thick with flowers. And never did Khosrow and Shirin leave one another's sight. In the mornings they would summon their attendants; then Shabdiz and Golgun would be led from the stable and they would ride to the polo field or to the hunt. Chasing after birds and game, Khosrow was astonished at the prowess of Shirin; her skill with the bow and her mastery of her horses's reins matched that of any man. She was a lioness, not a gazelle, and his heart pursued her eagerly. Yet at night when the dancing began, so light was her step that she seemed never to touch the ground.

Every night there were sumptuous feasts. Scarcely was one banquet finished

MINIATURE 2   *King Khosrow seated on his throne*

than the next began, and each was embellished with music, song, and wine, and poetry in praise of love. One evening, while gentle breezes wafted through the palace and cooled the heat of day, Shirin with ten attendants gathered at the foot of Khosrow's throne; each maiden recited poetry praising the love of Khosrow and Shirin. Then Shapur, who was among the company, told how he had awakened their love with his painting, and Shirin described the passion and amazement she had felt upon plucking the portrait from its bough. And Khosrow told the tale of a black lion that hunted a wild ass and was himself ensnared when the ass put a rope around his neck; thus was he, a powerful king, caught in the locks of Shirin's hair.

Now during these blissful days and nights Khosrow pleaded with Shirin to follow him to a secret place, an obscure corner of the court where they could talk of love and kiss, and not be seen. Mindful of her promise to the queen, Shirin resisted. Then, one evening, when they were walking unaccompanied in the palace gardens, Khosrow, flushed with wine, urged himself upon her with an overpowering embrace. Shirin rebuked him gently. "My love, we must not so forget ourselves in this enchanted garden that the garden of our future goes untended. Remember that you are a king, and a king deposed. If you would enjoy my bloom, salvage your good name, and let your state flower." And even as she spoke these words, Shirin was sweeter than all the roses in the arbor.

Thus was Khosrow spurred to action. Entrusting the welfare of his beloved to his faithful friend Shapur, he set out on Shabdiz the next morning for the kingdom of Byzantium. Without resting, he rode until he reached Constantinople, the great port city where the emperor had his residence. He went before that potentate and, pledging eternal friendship, asked for arms and men. Now the emperor paid heed, for he desired lasting peace with his powerful neighbor Persia. And when he ascertained from his astrologers that Khosrow's fortunes were on the rise, he agreed to give the young king a force of fifty thousand men. But the emperor was shrewd and required as a sign of their friendship that Khosrow marry his daughter Maryam and pledge that he would take no other wife besides.

Now Khosrow was sorely trapped. He loved Shirin beyond anything else on earth, and to enjoy her love he must redeem his crown. But how else could he regain his throne except by marriage to the Byzantine princess? He had his honor to avenge. Dreadful was his dilemma, for to pursue duty was to deny his love, and to deny duty was to deny his love as well. At last, with tortured heart, Khosrow consented to the contract, and to the joy of all Byzantium, the king of Persia and the princess Maryam were wed.

Immediately, the emperor mustered his army, and Niyatus was placed in command. They marched by night toward Persia. When the battle began, Khosrow

Detail from MINIATURE 2

went forth to meet Bahram Chubin accompanied by his adviser, the sage Bozorg Omid, who told him when to advance. The omens were auspicious, and the wicked Bahram Chubin was defeated; he fled toward China, and his men dispersed. Thus Khosrow regained his kingdom and was crowned in the capital city of Mada'in. There was great rejoicing throughout the land, but in his heart Khosrow could not rejoice, for he longed for Shirin. Sweeter than ever did she seem now, as sweet as the waters of life, and the days they had passed together seemed but a dream.

As Khosrow's fortunes changed, so did those of Shirin. Queen Mihin Banu had fallen ill, and soon breathed her last; the crown of Armenia was placed upon Shirin's unhappy head. She was desolate beyond description. She mourned the queen deeply, but even greater was her yearning for Khosrow. Shirin was filled with a longing that would not let her sleep.

Now Shirin was a just and gracious ruler; she abolished taxes, and her people prospered. Throughout the land perfect peace prevailed. The falcon drank together with the quail and the wolf lay with the lamb. Yet all the while her thoughts turned to Khosrow. When Shirin learned that Khosrow had regained his throne, she sent him many splendid gifts and asked every caravan for news of him. And then, with unbelieving ears, she heard of his marriage to the princess Maryam and his promise never to take another wife. Her unhappiness was so extreme that she could think of nothing else. Fearing that she would neglect her kingdom, she appointed a regent in her place and went with the faithful Shapur and a few attendants to the residence that had been built for her near Kermanshah, in Persia. Word of her arrival reached Khosrow. But the king, fearing Maryam's anger and her father's might, dared not go to her. Instead he sent for Shapur, and the good painter carried secret messages between the lovers.

Now in King Khosrow's court grand councils were held, followed by even grander feasts. One night, at a banquet, Khosrow drank too much wine and called for Barbad, the famous minstrel, to entertain the company. Barbad came before him and sang thirty songs about the love of Khosrow for Shirin and was rewarded by the king with jeweled robes and handsome gifts. So overwhelmed was Khosrow by the songs, and so emboldened by the wine, that he went to Maryam and told her that Shirin had left her kingdom for his sake and was languishing at her palace near Kermanshah. He asked Maryam to have Shirin brought to the palace Moshku as her slave. But Maryam was a jealous woman and refused, and vowed to kill Shirin should she ever see her. More than ever Khosrow longed to see Shirin, and so he sent Shapur to Shirin to beg her to meet him secretly in the palace Moshku; under cover of night, she was to slip past the gates—and Maryam's suspicious eye.

Shirin was indignant at so crass a plan. "Am I beneath the princess Maryam that I must crawl to Moshku in the dark?" she exclaimed. "Is Queen Shirin not as royal as Maryam and Khosrow? Khosrow has Shabdiz; if he would see me, let him ride to me!" And so she refused to go to Khosrow, and would speak no more of him.

Now the palace near Kermanshah, as we have said, was in an unhealthy place, and Shirin thirsted for milk. She would have pastured her own cows, but the fields near the palace were overgrown with poisonous weeds. One night, when she was conversing with the good Shapur, she spoke of her desire for milk, and the painter recalled one Farhad, a youth of great skill and cleverness, who had studied with Shapur in China, under the same drawing master. Now Farhad had mastered the works of Euclid on geometry and the treatise of Ptolemy on the stars, but his accomplishments in engineering and sculpture were even greater. So deftly did he carve as to make even the most obdurate stone sing with joy as he chipped it with his chisel. Moreover he was said to be as strong as two elephants and to have the muscles of a bull.

Farhad was summoned to the palace near Kermanshah. When he arrived, he stood patiently outside Shirin's quarters, with his loins girded, his massive arms widespread. At last Shirin appeared and told him of her need for milk. What was needed was a channel from a distant pasture, where flocks grazed, to the palace. In the far-off field shepherds could pour milk into the trough; it would flow to the palace, where Shirin's servants could draw it for her. As she spoke, Shirin's voice was so sweet that Farhad fell completely in love with her. He stood entranced, scarcely able to comprehend her words. Afterward, when all was explained to him, he took his axe and shovel and set out. Within a month the channel was finished, and in the rock by Shirin's door Farhad dug a pool which was already foaming with milk. When Shirin saw what he had done, she praised him greatly. Unclasping two pearls that dangled from her ears, she gave them to him. Farhad, overwhelmed, fled to the desert, where he wandered, weeping and calling Shirin's name. The wild beasts came to comfort him; the lion was his pillow and the wolf sat at his feet. But his longing for Shirin could not be eased.

Soon, word of Farhad's devotion to Shirin reached Khosrow's court, and Khosrow ordered Farhad brought to him. When Farhad appeared the king showered him with gold. But Farhad stood unmoved—so deep was his love for Shirin. Then Khosrow tested Farhad's love with severe questions, and he was astonished at the youth's determination. At last, Khosrow asked Farhad to cut a road through a grim and towering mountain that blocked a route he wished to travel. Farhad agreed, but only on the condition that if he succeeded, he be given Shirin as his reward. To this Khosrow consented, for so difficult was the task

that he was sure Farhad would fail. And so Farhad was taken to Mount Bisutun.

As soon as he arrived, Farhad took his axe and carved from the forbidding stone first an image of Shirin and then one of Khosrow riding on Shabdiz. The images finished, his fearful work began. He labored day and night; so steadfastly did he wield his axe that word of his prowess spread from mouth to mouth. Even as he worked, he became a legend throughout Persia. Indeed, he paused only to gaze upon the likeness of Shirin, to kiss its feet and moan and weep, or to climb to the mountain top and call out to Shirin and plead his love.

When Shirin heard of Farhad's feat, for there was none in all the land who did not speak of it, she marveled greatly and set out for Mount Bisutun. When he saw her, Farhad so lost his senses that with one hand he beat his chest while with the other he continued to carve the rock. Not knowing what help to offer nor what words to say, Shirin drew a flask of milk from her saddlebag and, with trembling hands, gave it to Farhad. He drank it all in one draught, but it only increased his passion. When Shirin made ready to depart, her horse, exhausted by the steep climb up the mountainside, stumbled at its first step. Farhad lifted both horse and rider onto his shoulders and did not set them down again until he reached the gate of Shirin's residence. He returned to Bisutun, and worked with such ferocity that the road was soon nearly completed.

Khosrow, who kept close watch on his beloved, learned of Shirin's visit to Bisutun and of Farhad's progress. Greatly alarmed at the thought of Farhad completing his task, he summoned his advisers. The eldest of them, a cunning man, counseled him thus: "Magnificence, what is the true purpose of that youth's exertions but to win the heart and hand of the beautiful Shirin? What would he do if he were to learn that that heart had stopped and that hand was stilled by a mortal illness?"

And so a messenger was sent to Mount Bisutun, where he found Farhad cleaving the rock. "Why do you toil your life away like this, among these rocks, my friend?" he asked. "A strong young man like you should wield his chisel on a maiden!"

"I work for my king and for my love," Farhad replied with not a smile and not a break in the rhythm of his axe.

"And who might this love be?"

"Queen Shirin it is I love, for whom I have no words but my labors. Nor have I one more word for you!"

"Queen Shirin! Have you not heard? Shirin is dead but yesterday, taken by a fever. All her palace howls with grief!"

Without a word, Farhad flung away his axe so savagely that the blade split and quivered in the rock. He moaned and for the last time declared his love,

MINIATURE 3 *Shirin visits Farhad on the mountain*

for then he threw himself from Mount Bisutun to his death. Now the axe of Farhad had a handle of pomegranate wood, and in the very place where it landed, the handle took root and sprouted into a tree. And even to this day, on the branches of that tree, fruit does grow.

When Shirin learned of Farhad's death, her grief was great. As time passed, she mourned more deeply still, for she understood how true Farhad had been. And she caused a dome to be built over his grave as a place of pilgrimage for faithful lovers. For his part, Khosrow was so tortured with remorse that he did not know a moment's peace. At last he sent a letter to Shirin, lamenting Farhad's fate and soothing her sorrow by reminding her that no one is immortal. Shirin joyfully kissed the letter in three places, and pondered every word. But soon she turned from Khosrow, knowing in her heart that he had crafted the destruction of Farhad.

Now it happened, shortly afterward, that the king's consort Maryam became ill and died. Khosrow wore robes of black and withdrew from his court, but he mourned only for display. In secret he rejoiced; no longer was he bound by his promise to the emperor of Byzantium. Shirin mourned for the princess for the time prescribed, for such was the duty of everyone in the land, but after a long while sent a reply to Khosrow's letter. Gently she reminded the king that there is good and bad in life, weddings and deaths, and now that Maryam was dead, there would be other brides for him. Khosrow, she tenderly wrote, should overcome his grief and take another wife. Whereupon Khosrow sent a messenger to tell Shirin that he would marry her at last.

But this was not to be, for while they were exchanging messages, Khosrow passed his time in feasting and enjoyment. All the rulers of the world came to his court to pay him homage. And one day, surrounded by splendid company, he playfully inquired as to where the most beautiful women in the world were to be found. The strongest claim was for the Persian city of Isfahan and for the beauty Shekar. The charms of Shekar were vividly described to him, yet for a year Khosrow waited, unsure of his desires. At last he saddled Shabdiz and set out for Isfahan. He was well received at Shekar's residence; a banquet was set, musicians played, and the lovely Shekar was brought to amuse him. Khosrow was entranced. But when, nodding from the wine, he was led to his chamber, Shekar sent one of her handmaidens in her place. The next morning the girl reported to her mistress that Khosrow was unpleasing only in the sourness of his breath. Thereupon the playful Shekar revealed her trick to Khosrow and ordered him to return in a year's time; meanwhile he was to eat only certain foods.

In a year's time Khosrow dutifully returned and again, when night came, Shekar played her trick. At dawn she sent for him and told him that no man had yet enjoyed her love. Khosrow went into the streets of Isfahan, and when he learned from the people that Shekar had spoken truly, he brought her to his capital as his bride. Such comfort did the beautiful Shekar provide that Khosrow soon forgot his realm and his love for Shirin.

When Shirin first heard of this, she hid her sorrow; as the gardener tends his flowers, so did she cultivate indifference. But for all her pretenses, her grief took hold like a tenacious weed, and she soon gave in to despair. The name of Khosrow was forbidden in her presence, and so troubled was she that she could not sleep. Each night seemed like a year; from sundown until daybreak she would pray to God to release her from her plight. At last her prayers were answered. In a short time Khosrow tired of his new companion, and once again began to think of Shirin.

One day Khosrow ordered a royal hunt of unsurpassed splendor to be arranged. Among his entourage were the emperor of China and the commander of the armies of Byzantium. Before them went youths, leading horses and scattering incense. Guards had been brought from far-off lands, and they rode on elephants. Musicians played drums and pipes, and banners flapped in the breeze. When it came time to hunt, the king's prize falcons were released, and within a week the fields and forests were despoiled of partridges and quail. Then Khosrow left the company and started toward Shirin's palace. It was winter, and the night was cold. He ordered a fire made from precious scented woods, and in the morning he warmed himself with several cups of wine. As he drank he stirred with longing, and sent a messenger ahead to tell Shirin's court of his arrival; he rode on in haste.

When word of Khosrow's approach reached the palace, Shirin had all the doors locked. Then she stationed attendants at the gate, and gave each a tray filled with gold coins to scatter before Khosrow. She caused a path to be made of carpets and embroidered cloths, and set attendants in readiness to burn aloe-wood when the king at last arrived. Then Shirin went to the roof of her palace to watch for him. First she saw dust, then Khosrow's companions, then Khosrow himself, carrying white narcissus, her favorite flower. At the sight of him in the distance, she fainted, but recovered quickly and retired to her chamber.

Khosrow was welcomed with great festivity. Gold was showered; silks were spread; tents were raised and covered with jeweled canopies. And in the largest tent of all stood a golden, six-legged throne especially for Khosrow. He was a joyful king as he triumphantly approached the palace door. But when he tried to enter he was amazed to find it locked. He questioned all who stood around and sent a message to Shirin, telling her that he had come to beg forgiveness at her feet, and he would remain in the courtyard until she showed herself to him.

Shirin replied that she would only speak to him from her roof. Then she put on her finest robes and returned to the roof. When Khosrow saw her, he was so overcome that he kissed the ground. He praised her gifts—the gold, the silks, the throne—then reproached her for locking the door against him. Was this the way to treat an honored guest, no less a king?

Torn between desire and anger, Shirin wished Khosrow welcome with queenly dignity. But then desire succumbed to anger, and she bitterly described the sufferings she had endured. She reproached him for coming to her merry with wine. If he sought love, he must be sober and take her as his wife. If he sought only pleasure, let him return to Shekar and never come to her palace again. Thus they quarreled, Khosrow repenting and pleading the excesses of youth, Shirin thinking of her dishonor and of the faithful Farhad. What had Khosrow done to prove his love? With words as hard as ice she berated him, and at last in great despair he left the palace. Seeking sweetness he had found only bitterness. In the cold rain and snow he rode back through the forest to his hunting party. When he reached his tent he ordered his attendants to leave him alone with his sorrow and the faithful Shapur, who had followed him from Shirin's castle. All night long Khosrow was restless; he told Shapur that he still loved Shirin and the painter replied that lovers' quarrels are more show than substance. "What beauty is won with ease? Does not a rose have thorns? Take heart, my king! Fortune is good, and in the end all will be well!"

Now as she watched Khosrow depart, Shirin felt deep remorse, and wept. That night she saddled Golgun and, following the tracks of Shabdiz through the woods, found her way to Khosrow's camp. At the sound of hooves, Shapur ran out—the guards were drunk and sleeping—and helped Shirin dismount. She told him of her change of heart and asked two things: first, that Shapur hide her in the camp until such time as she should decide to show herself to Khosrow, and second, that Shapur was to help her return in safety to her palace if Khosrow refused to marry her. Shapur agreed; he tethered Golgun, hid Shirin, and returned to Khosrow's tent.

The king slept fitfully, and when he awoke he told Shapur that he had dreamt he was in a beautiful garden with a beautiful maiden at his side. Shapur told him that the maiden surely was Shirin, and that they would soon be reunited. In the meantime, Khosrow should celebrate this good omen with festivities. And so, the next day, as the sun descended from the sky, Khosrow called forth his cup-bearers and close attendants and drank and scattered gold. Then he dismissed all but Shapur and summoned the spell-binding musician Barbad.

Now there was in Khosrow's camp a second musician of unsurpassing skill. And Shirin asked Shapur to bring Nikisa, for this was his name, to the tent in

which she hid and to station him outside so that she could whisper instructions from within. "Let me direct him in my heart's true measures, while Barbad gives voice to Khosrow," she said.

So it was that the lovers conversed in song. Their music was as clear as the cold night air; each word shone like a star. First Nikisa sang for Shirin: she would not be a slave to Khosrow, yet her fury had been tempered and she would show sweetness to him. To which Barbad repled by pledging Khosrow's eternal love. Then Nikisa sang of loneliness: better for Shirin to die than live without Khosrow. In turn, Barbad bewailed Shirin's locked door; if she would come to Khosrow, he would make her his queen and never leave her side.

As Barbad sang, Khosrow was overwhelmed and spoke above the playing of the harp. He asked a hundred times for forgiveness and spoke so movingly of his devotion that Shirin, unable to restrain herself, cried out. When he heard her voice, Khosrow ran toward the tent in which she hid; she came forth, and he tried to embrace her. But Shirin drew back, reminding Khosrow that she would not be his until she was his wife. Then Khosrow ordered a marriage settlement be drafted; while this was being done, they would celebrate together. Shirin became insensible with happiness; she was so joyful and so lovely that Khosrow was enraptured, and he could not stop gazing on her beauty. For seven days did his eyes feast on her. Then Shirin went back to her palace riding in a golden litter, and Khosrow returned to the capital of Meda'in to make ready for the wedding. The royal astrologers scanned the heavens for auspicious omens and, after much deliberation, fixed upon a day. Then Khosrow sent a caravan of camels and horses laden with precious gifts to Shirin to bring her back. He summoned all his nobles and told them that Shirin would be his wife at last. They rejoiced and a splendid marriage took place on the appointed day.

No sooner had Khosrow and Shirin exchanged their vows and invoked God's blessing than the blue of the sky deepened to purple with the coming of night, and there was revelry throughout the land. The feasting and drinking at the royal palace was greater than ever before. The musicians Barbad and Nikisa played their harps until the early hours of the morning. Then, as the heavens began to lighten, Khosrow was carried to the bridal chamber to which Shirin, long wearied of the festivities, had withdrawn. When she saw that Khosrow was dazed by wine, she was angered and sent a wrinkled, hairy, hunchbacked old womanservant to him. It was a crone whom Khosrow took in his eager embrace; a crow in place of a beauty, a dragon instead of the moon. The king cried out and cursed, and threw her from the chamber. Shirin, well satisfied that Khosrow was not beyond his senses, dismissed the servant and went in to him.

As dawn broke, the lovers were united in a perfect love. The strength of the lion mingled with the sweetness of the rose. All that day and night, and even the next, and the day and night after that, they lingered within, until at last their joy was spent. Then Khosrow again sat on his throne, and all around him shared in his good fortune. He gave a great estate and the choice of Shirin's handmaidens for a bride to the faithful Shapur. And the good sage Bozorg Omid and the musicians Barbad and Nikisa were given brides as well.

For many years the reign of Khosrow and Shirin was a happy one. Khosrow was just, and his subjects knew prosperity, peace, and glory. The prophecy of his grandfather Khosrow Anushirvan was fulfilled, for Khosrow now possessed the four things promised him: the black stallion Shabdiz, the world's swiftest steed, was in his stable; Taqdis, the throne of thrones, covered with precious jewels, stood in his palace; in his banquet-hall played the musician Barbad, who with the touch of his harpstring surpassed all other minstrels, and at his side was his destined love, Shirin.

But fate is fickle, and in time the wheel of fortune turned. It so happened that a son had been born to Khosrow and the princess Maryam, and at the hour of his birth the signs were such that the astrologers shook their heads and sighed. Shiruyeh, as he was named, grew up just as the heavens foretold, a surly child and a stranger to his father. Even as a boy Shiruyeh plotted to seize the throne that one day would rightfully be his. Perceiving evil in his heart, Khosrow had thought to kill him, but he was restrained only by the wise Bozorg Omid, who counseled, "Might it not be, Magnificence, that from bad comes good? Who can know God's will?"

And so it came to pass that one day while Khosrow was praying, the wicked Shiruyeh invaded the palace with his forces and claimed the throne. Khosrow was put in chains and cast into a dungeon, and Shirin voluntarily went to prison with him. Great was Khosrow's grief, though Shirin comforted him gently day and night. In the darkness, for the thick stone walls would admit not a single ray of sun, she would remind him that there is both good and evil in the world. Fortunes rise and fall; all things change. "The only constant in life," she said, "is inconstancy itself." Then she spoke of love and told him stories of the kind that close the eyes of anxious children. As he slept she paced back and forth to stay awake; for she was afraid that harm would come to them if they were both to sleep.

One night, as Khosrow slept, so weary was Shirin that she succumbed to sleep. It was a strange, eerie night, for not one star could be seen. And it was this night that a treacherous assassin crept into the dungeon through a chink in the stone wall, and made his way to Khosrow's cell. With his dagger, the killer stabbed

Khosrow in the liver, and ran off. Khosrow awoke to find himself wounded and close to death. He thirsted for water but would not disturb Shirin, for he knew how tired she was. The blood flowed from his wound, and without the slightest motion or whisper, Khosrow breathed his last.

Disturbed by the wetness of the blood-soaked robes, Shirin awoke. When she saw Khosrow, her heart went numb with sorrow, and she wept for hours on end. Then she asked her jailers for musk and camphor so that she could bathe Khosrow's body.

Now at the time Khosrow and Shirin were wed, Shiruyeh was only a boy. But even so, he lusted for Shirin, and ever since, he desired his father's wife as greedily as he coveted his father's throne. And so he sent a messenger to the dungeon to ask Shirin to marry him, promising her a life of luxury and ease. Shirin consented but requested first that all Khosrow's possessions be distributed among the poor. When this had been done, a golden bier was brought, and Khosrow's body was placed on it, and he was buried with great splendor. In the streets of the city Meda'in the people wept as the body was carried past. Kings and emperors came from distant lands, as far-off even as the Orient, to march in the funeral procession. And among them all went Shirin, dressed not in mourning but, to the astonishment of all, in robes of red and yellow.

When the procession reached the vault that housed the royal tombs, the bier was carried inside. Shirin followed and asked that she be left alone to say farewell to Khosrow and to think fondly of her future happiness. Shiruyeh, flushed with love and triumph, readily agreed. Shirin entered the vault, locked the door, and went to Khosrow's side. She covered him with kisses and, with a dagger she had hidden in her robes, fatally stabbed herself in the same place where Khosrow had been stabbed.

Now it is said by some that when her blood flowed over Khosrow's body, he awakened for a moment and the lovers kissed. Yet others say that Khosrow stirred not from his timeless sleep, but that the stars paused in their celestial course in stark amazement at a love so fine.

When all who were outside the vault learned of what has passed within, a great wailing arose and a year's mourning was decreed throughout the land of Persia. Shirin was buried beside her beloved, and above their graves an inscription was carved as a memorial to all who love. Thus were Khosrow and Shirin united for all eternity. And their story has been told and told again, and has become a legend, an inspiration to all lovers faithful and true, from that time to this very day.

Detail from MINIATURE 4

COMMENTARY

Khosrow and Shirin

"Khosrow and Shirin" is the second poem of Nizami's *Khamseh* and the first of his romantic epics. Its protagonists are Khosrow II, the last great Sasanian monarch, known as Parviz, the Victorious, and his mistress Shirin; their love was recorded by many historians, geographers, and travelers, among them the Muslims Tabari (Bal'ami), Ibn Rustah, Ibn al-Faqih, Yaqut, and the anonymous compiler of the *Compendium of History*. There are many descriptions of Khosrow's palace at Ctesiphon, the palace of Shirin, and especially the grotto rock-carving at Taq-e Bustan, the figures of which were early associated in history and legend with Khosrow II, Shirin, and sometimes the engineer Farhad. The beautiful equestrian sculpture was said to be Khosrow mounted on the horse Shabdiz.[1] These archeological sites are located in close proximity along the ancient trade route to China, at the point where the plain of Mesopotamia meets the Iranian plateau.

According to these and other sources, the long and turbulent reign of Khosrow Parviz (590–628 A.D.) was characterized by a high, though ultimately exhausting, degree of military glory and courtly splendor. In return for political and military assistance against the usurper Bahram Chubin, Khosrow ceded part of Armenia to the Emperor of Byzantium and was married to his daughter Maryam. Although Nizami portrays Shirin as an Armenian princess, chroniclers did not consider her of royal blood. The name Shirin is a Persian word meaning sweet, and she has been variously claimed by Khuzistan and Syria.

Secondary figures in the epic also have some historical basis. The engineering feats of the herculean Farhad appear in several of the sources; and Barbad and Nikisa were the chief musicians at Khosrow's court. Khosrow's fabulous horse Shabdiz is also mentioned frequently.

The love of Khosrow and Shirin was early a popular subject with poets. Less than one hundred years after Khosrow's death, the Arab poet Khalid ibn Fayyaz wrote of their romance. According to literary tradition, the first Persian love couplets were engraved on the walls of Shirin's palace and were still legible and revered three centuries after she died. The wonders of the horse Shabdiz also figure in many ancient stories.

The great Ferdowsi devoted more than four thousand couplets to Khosrow II's reign in his *Shah-nameh*, or *Book of Kings*, composed at the end of the tenth and the beginning of the eleventh century A.D. In this account, from which Nizami drew his inspiration, the youthful Khosrow took Shirin as his mistress and forgot her when he became king. Later, while on the way to hunting, he saw her on the terrace of her house and was again enflamed by her beauty. Despite opposition from the aristocracy and religious leaders because she was a commoner, they were married. Shirin then secretly poisoned Khosrow's first wife, the Byzantine princess Maryam. This dreadful act embittered Khosrow and Maryam's son Shiruyeh and, afraid of retaliation, Khosrow imprisoned him. When, in a military coup, Shiruyeh was freed, he in turn imprisoned Khosrow and had him assassinated. He spared Shirin only because he wanted her as his wife. Shirin agreed to marry her stepson, but she demanded that she retain control of her inherited wealth and that she be allowed to mourn at Khosrow's tomb. After distributing her assets among the poor and the temples and contributing to the construction of inns for travelers, she went to the grave, took strong poison, and died at Khosrow's side.

Khosrow, Shirin, and Farhad are also celebrated in the poetry of Qatran, the eleventh-century court poet of Tabriz and Ganjeh. In the same era, Gurgani explored various aspects of love and passion in his *Vis and Ramin*, using an historical-legendary theme from ancient Eastern Iran. But Nizami was the first to fulfill all the prerequisites of romance—far-off times and places, with giants, dragons, and heroic exploits; sentimental and idealistic exaggerations that still preserved the individual events so dear to the Near Eastern reader; and reflection on the human condition.

Most important, Nizami gave this material a real structural unity. Infusing the story with his own profound experience of love and expanding it with his thoughts on religion, philosophy, and government, he created a romance of great dramatic intensity. The story has a constant forward drive with exposition, challenge, mystery, crisis, climax, resolution, and, finally, catastrophe. The action increases in complexity as the protagonists face mounting complications. For instance, Khosrow and Shirin are not able to meet for a long time, despite their untiring efforts and the help of their confidant. Then, after they do meet, they are forced apart by the political marriage of Khosrow and Maryam. When Khosrow promises Shirin to Farhad as a prize for completing a feat of daring and endurance, the story nearly comes to a premature conclusion.

After the death of Maryam and the murder-suicide of Farhad, it seems that all obstacles are removed and the lovers will be united. But Nizami introduces an affair between Khosrow and a girl from Isfahan that further complicates and delays his union with Shirin. Finally, on the lovers' wedding night, Nizami creates a bizarre episode, a humorous entr'act that gives the reader or listener a chance to take a deep breath before the epic's tragic climax. Khosrow gets drunk and Shirin replaces her presence in the nuptial chamber with that of a knotty, wizened old crone. Through these dramatic devices Nizami makes a powerful commentary on human behavior, on its follies, its glories, its struggles, and its unbridled passions and tragedies.

Nizami's deep understanding of women is strongly expressed in "Khosrow and Shirin." Shirin is the central character and there is no question that she is a poetic tribute to Nizami's wife Afaq. She is well-educated, independent, fearless, resourceful, imaginative, erotic, and humorous. Her loyalty knows no bounds. That she is a queen rather than a commoner gives the story a stately quality. Her association with Armenia is, perhaps, a reflection of its geographical proximity to Ganjeh.

Shirin, like the Byzantine Maryam, was a Christian. Nizami was a pious Muslim, but he tolerated and respected other religions.

Shirin's sense of justice is so great that she forswears Khosrow's love until he should regain his throne, thus fulfilling his responsibility to his people. Even after they are married she continues to exert a strong influence on Khosrow, educating him as always through example and love. As a result the country flourished, justice was observed and strengthened, and science, religion, and philosophy thrived.[2]

Shirin is democratic, companionable with the faithful painter-messenger Shapur and sensible of the depth of Farhad's wordless devotion. Though she is prey to jealousy and loneliness, she is master of her passions and is capable of the ultimate renunciation, death for love.[3]

In contrast, Khosrow is governed by his predilection for sumptuous living and personal expediency. He is selfish and vacillating. He basely tricks Farhad, forcing him wittingly to suicide. However, when he comes upon Shirin bathing in a wilderness pool, he chivalrously averts his eyes; and when he knows that his end is near, rather than wake the exhausted Shirin, he allows himself to bleed to death in silence. Nizami portrays this final act in such a way that it becomes a remission of Khosrow's previous sins.

The tension between the strength of Shirin and the weakness of Khosrow is enhanced dramatically by Nizami's tight control of plot and setting, and in his development of the towering figure of Farhad. Episodes of meeting and of missing, of searching and of waiting, are richly entwined with scenes of the barren desert and of luxurious court life. Asceticism vies with sensuality.

Nizami's use of allegories, parables, and words with double meaning raised the Persian language to a new height. Though always pure, Nizami's poetry is elaborate and flamboyant, playing on all the senses at once. The poem is written in the light, flowing, graceful *Hazaj mussadas maqsur* meter, deliberately imitating that used by Gurgani in *Vis and Ramin*. It scans as follows:

∪ − − − / ∪ − − − / ∪ − − // ∪ − − − / ∪ − − − / ∪ − −

There are about 6,500 couplets.

Composed after the mystico-didactic *Makhzan al-*

Asrar, its exact date of completion is uncertain. The year 576 A.H./1180 A.D. is given in some manuscripts, but many scholars believe, because of internal evidence, that it was finished after 581 A.H./1184 A.D. In an autobiographical passage woven into the text, Nizami says that he has lived for forty years. That must be construed as a conventional number, but, in any case, scholars disagree by six years, from 535–541 A.H./1140–1146 A.D., as to the date of his birth. Nor are the three dedicatory invocations—to Sultan Tughrol II and to his regents, Atabeg Muhammad Jahan Pahlavan and Atabeg Qizil Arslan—useful in establishing a secure date. Although Atabeg Muhammad Jahan Pahlavan was the ruler of Ganjeh where Nizami lived, and Atabeg Qizil Arslan gave Nizami title to a village, these dedications may well have been added by Nizami for political reasons or may be later interpolations. The earliest extant text, dating from 763 A.H./1362 A.D., was written some one hundred and fifty years after Nizami's death and is suspected to contain many apocryphal verses.[4]

Nizami may have written "Khosrow and Shirin" to express his happiness during his marriage to Afaq, but the idealization of womanly chastity, purity, and devotion, the recurrent theme of renunciation, and the tragic ending make it seem more probable that it was written as a memorial to her after her untimely death. Its passages instructing their son Muhammad in the ways of virtue may possibly be interpreted as a sign of Nizami's strong affection and concern for a motherless boy. These exhortations are contained mainly in the postscripts in which Nizami muses about the transiency and vanity of life on earth. Only religion is sure. As part of the conclusion, Nizami relates a dream Khosrow had about the prophet Muhammad, toward the end of his reign; it had such an impact on the king that he could not sleep for several months.

The great Persian authority on Nizami, Vahid Dastgerdi, calls "Khosrow and Shirin" "the best historical fable of love and chastity, the treasure of eloquence, counsel, and wisdom."[5] The foremost Russian specialist, E. É. Bertels, believes that "Khosrow and Shirin" is "one of the great masterpieces, not only in the Azarbaijani but in world literature. For the first time in the poetry of the Near East, the personality of a human being has been shown with all its richness, with all its contradictions and ups and downs."[6] J. Rypka in his comprehensive study of Iranian literature writes of "Khosrow and Shirin": "It is the story of the love and sorrow of a princess and a woman and a wife, in its sincerity unequaled by any other work in Persian literature."[7]

In this volume we are presenting the first English version of Nizami's "Khosrow and Shirin."

1. This rock-carving, situated some six miles northeast of the city of Kermanshah, is still not definitely identified and dated. It represents a royal investiture, a common artistic theme during the Sasanian period.

2. At last Khosrow finds time to pursue his interest in philosophy, science, and religion. With his mentor, Bozorg Omid, he discusses the questions that have occupied the Persian mind for centuries: Where do we come from? What are we here for? Where do we go? They examine the characteristics of the earth and climate, and the formation of the universe. As Khosrow II was a contemporary of the prophet Muhammad, they discuss Islam and his philosopher-adviser urges him to look upon it as God's true revelation. The historical Khosrow was a Zoroastrian, the national religion of the Sasanian Empire.

3. The Russian scholar E. É. Bertels gives an interesting interpretation of Shirin as a victim of her own fate. Her idealization of her beloved leads to disappointment when it undergoes the test of reality. The strength of Shirin lies in her rising above disenchantment, in her persistent belief that one day Khosrow will measure up to her heroic imagination. See E. É. Bertels, *Nizami, Tvorcheskiy Put Poeta* (Moscow, 1956), p.123.

4. E. É. Bertels (op cit., p. 103) and J. Rypka (*The Cambridge History of Iran*, Cambridge University Press, 1968, vol. 5, p. 580) think that "Khosrow and Shirin" was commissioned by Sultan Tughrol II, who asked for a romantic poem without being specific about its theme. In the postscript to "Khosrow and Shirin" there is praise of Atabeg Qizil Arslan, who feted Nizami when he was in the vicinity of Ganjeh. Nizami was not a court poet, but this tribute made him very happy. He describes in detail the respect and kindness with which he was received by the ruler. This postscript is a later addition because the poem which Atabeg Qizil Arslan thought so highly of was "Khosrow and Shirin."

5. Vahid Dastgerdi, critical edition of "Khosrow and Shirin" (Tehran, 1933), p.1.

6. E. É. Bertels, *Nizami, Tvorcheskiy Put Poeta* (Moscow, 1956), p. 124.

7. J. Rypka, *History of Iranian Literature* (Dordrecht: D. Reidel, 1968), p.211.

Layla and Majnun

Long ago, in the desert of Arabia, lived many great chieftains, and the greatest was the chieftain of the tribe of the Banu Amir. Now this *sayyid*, as he was reverently called, had wealth beyond imagining; his gold and jewels were as countless as the grains of desert sand, and in his tent hung the most precious silks and carpets, and the finest herds grazed upon his land. But rich as he was in worldly goods, he was richer still in the goodness of his heart. He ruled with perfect justice and was generous to all; to those in need he readily opened his purse, and every traveler was welcome in his camp. His tribesmen prospered, and they loved and honored him. The *sayyid* was well content, but for one thing: he had no son and heir.

As the years passed and no son was born, he prayed to God with all his heart and brooded on the fortune that denied to him what he most desired. "What care I for my jewels and gold if I should die without an heir?" he asked. "Indeed, he truly lives who lives in the memory of his son!" And thus he prayed even more fervently, until, at last, his prayers were answered, and God gave to him a son.

There was great celebration in the camp of the Banu Amir, and the *sayyid* opened his treasury so that all might share in his happiness. The desert was filled with shouts of joy, for the child was a boy of unsurpassing handsomeness, even from the very moment of his birth. When he was but two weeks old, his face was as round and as beaming as the moon, and every year his comeliness increased. And the good *sayyid* was known to exclaim, "Of all men on this earth, surely none is more fortunate than I!"

Now when Qays, for so the boy was named, was of school age, he was sent to study under a learned teacher. So quick of mind was he that scarcely did he take a pen in hand than he had mastered script; no sooner did he hold a book than he could read. He was eager for new knowledge, and in all the learned disciplines he excelled, but his greatest skill by far was in the art of discourse. When he spoke, his words were sweeter than the music of a lute; his wit sharper than an arrow; his wisdom more lustrous than a pearl. All his schoolmates gathered round and listened with delight.

Now the pupils in this school were from the noblest families, and so it was that one morning the daughter of a mighty chieftain, second only to the *sayyid* himself, was brought into the classroom. This little girl was very beautiful. She was as slender as a cypress tree and as graceful as a bird; her skin was white as milk, her cheeks and lips were red as roses, and she had the darting black eyes of a gazelle. But even darker than her eyes was her raven hair; her hair was more lustrous than the sky at midnight, and indeed she was called Layla, or Night.

The moment Layla came into the schoolroom love awakened in Qays' heart. All that day he could neither read nor write, but only stare at her and wonder at her beauty and at her long black hair. Enraptured, he whispered "Layla, Layla," softly as if in prayer, and all the next day, and the next, and for many days after, he could say no word but "Layla!" Even at this tender age, Qays claimed her for his own and vowed that he would love her all his life.

And Layla loved Qays in return. Yet they spoke not, for their souls were so perfectly attuned that they had no need of words. Thus Qays would gaze at Layla while the other pupils studied or played in the courtyard. And Layla would blush deeply, lower her lashes, then open her eyes and gaze at him and sweetly smile. And every evening, when the sun set and the heavens darkened and the two were apart, they sighed and wept and eagerly went to their beds, all the sooner to dream of one another. When the sun rose they would hasten joyfully to school. Thus did they love, and every day their love increased.

Now love shines more brightly even than the sun, and Qays loved Layla so intensely that after a while the other children noticed what was plain to see. They were too young to know of love, and so they laughed at Qays and pointed at him, and cried, "Our friend has lost his heart and head! He cares not for his books but thinks only of Layla. See how he stares at her like a love-stricken sheep!"

Then Qays tried to hide his love, but his eyes refused to stray from Layla's face. His schoolmates would follow him taunting, "Have you not heard that Qays loves Layla? Like a madman he stares at her, and chants her name!"

At last Qays could contain himself no longer and surrendered to his passion. In the classroom, as the others recited their lessons, he shouted "Layla! Layla!" And he ran through the streets and the bazaars, calling out her name, praising her black eyes and her raven hair. People looked after him and shook their heads. "Indeed, he is a madman, a *majnun*," they said. And so it was that Qays came to be called Majnun.

Now it was not long before word of Majnun's infatuation reached the ears of Layla's father, and the chieftain was greatly incensed. "Who is this Majnun,

MINIATURE 5   *Layla and Majnun at school*

that he should speak Layla's name in the bazaars and thus insult my daughter and my tribe?" And so the chieftain ordered that Layla be taken from the school at once and brought to the desert camp and confined in a tent alone.

Majnun was sick at heart. For several days he sat listlessly before his open books, staring sadly at her empty place. When he could no longer bear Layla's absence, he closed his books and fled to the bazaars. From dawn to dusk he wandered among the stalls, murmuring her name and sobbing with grief. So deeply did he suffer, and so strongly did he love, that his ravings became poems. Walking in the markets, Majnun, the possessed, composed love songs of the most exquisite beauty. And as he sang, the wind lifted his words, like leaves, and carried them into the desert. "Layla, Layla! May my songs fall at your feet!" he cried.

And every night, when darkness fell, Majnun followed his songs into the desert. With two or three faithful companions who were still his friends, he crept into the camp of Layla's tribe. Approaching her tent, he hid behind a tree, hoping for a glimpse of his beloved. One night Layla, restless and sleepless, sat at the door of her tent. Majnun suddenly appeared. In the moonlight they gazed at one another, unbelievingly and trembling with love; neither could say a word. It was not until the sky reddened with dawn that Majnun turned and hastened back to his own camp lest he be discovered.

From that day on, his passion burned even more fiercely; like a thorn-bush set afire Majnun was consumed by love. And as he lost his heart, so he lost his reason. Leaving the camp of the Banu Amir, he wandered in the desert and the mountains of Najd. And as he went he tore his robes, shouted Layla's name, and wildly sang his songs. He went alone, for his friends despaired of him and left. From afar people would point to him and say, "There goes Majnun, that madman who was once called Qays. For love of Layla does he wander in the wilderness and bring dishonor on his father and his tribe."

Now when Majnun fled into the wilderness, the good *sayyid* grieved greatly. He called his counselors to him. "Indeed, my son has lost his heart," he said. "His senses are confused, for without Layla does he live in darkness. If he should win her, surely he will find his light." And thus did the *sayyid* resolve to go to Layla's father and ask the chieftain for her hand. The next morning, as the sun rose in the sky, a search party went into the desert to find Majnun. At the same time the *sayyid* set out for Layla's camp. His camels were laden with many precious gifts, and his hopes were brighter even than the rising sun.

But when he went before the chieftain and told why he had come, the chieftain spoke harshly, for he was a proud man. "Who has not heard of Majnun's madness?" he declared. "My daughter will not marry him! See first that your son is cured, then come to me again. For even if I were to grant your wish, as surely as the sun beats down upon the desert sand, Layla's name will soon again be heard in the bazaars, and every man in all Arabia will laugh at me!"

The *sayyid* sadly shook his head and returned to his own camp. There he found Majnun, and told his son what Layla's father had said. "Why must you worship only Layla?" he asked. "Indeed, among our tribe there are a thousand lovely maidens. Choose one as your wife, and forget Layla. Then you will be happy!"

But Majnun only cried out in despair and fled once more into the wilderness. He stumbled across the burning sand, thorns caught at his robes, and still he called "Layla! Layla!" And he tore at his hair and sung his songs until the desert resounded with his words. As he passed through one village and then another, all who heard him marveled at his eloquence; they pitied him and wept. Yet Majnun saw them not, nor did he hear their weeping, or even the sound of his own voice, for he could think only of Layla. At last, like a burnt-out candle, he fell exhausted to his knees and, whispering Layla's name once more, prayed to God for death. "I am an outcast. I bring only shame upon my tribe. Let me die now, for there is no hope for me in life!" Thus he sighed and sank onto the sand.

No sooner had he fainted than a group of shepherds gathered. They prepared a litter for him and carried him gently across the desert to the camp of the Banu Amir. There he lay in his own tent singing his songs and calling Layla's name. And his father's sorrow was no less than Majnun's. "Would that Majnun had never set eyes on Layla, for no longer do I have a son!" he lamented.

With a heavy heart, he called his counselors to him once more. To the eldest he said, "Does not the whole world go to Mecca, to ask God's blessing? Let us, too, make a pilgrimage, and pray to God that Majnun should be cured."

And so it was that in the month of pilgrimage, the last month of the year, the *sayyid* and his closest kinsmen departed from their camp and traveled to Mecca. For this journey the *sayyid* chose his best camels. A litter was devised for Majnun, and as the caravan crossed the desert, Majnun was carried as gently as if he were an infant in his cradle. At last they entered Mecca, and the *sayyid* showered gold coins, as alms, upon the crowds of people in the streets. Then, trembling with hope, he brought Majnun before the shrine, and, taking his hand, said softly, "My son, ask God to save you from your passion; pray to Him to end your madness. Surely you will be cured."

When Majnun heard these words, he wept bitterly. Then he laughed wildly and stretched out his hands toward the shrine, the Kaaba. In supplication, he touched the shrine. "I pray to You, let me not be cured of love, but let my passion grow!" he cried. "Take what is left of my life and give it to Layla's,

yet let me never demand from her so much as a single hair! Let me love for love's sake, and make my love a hundred times as great as it is this very day!"

As Majnun so prayed the *sayyid* listened silently and bowed his head with grief. Then they returned to their camp. When they arrived, the *sayyid* told his kinsmen, "I have tried, but never will Majnun be cured, for before the holy Kaaba he has blessed Layla and cursed himself."

Now everyone in the city of Mecca heard of Majnun's prayer, and there was none in the land of Arabia who did not speak of it. When word reached the camp of Layla's tribe, the chieftain thundered with rage and vowed to kill Majnun. But first he sent two messengers to the court of the sultan to register his complaint. "Magnificence," they said, "this Majnun is a man possessed and does dishonor to our tribe. Order him to be punished at once, so that the name of Layla will be unstained."

Then the sultan's prefect drew his sword. "So be it; let him be punished as you wish."

Now it happened that a kinsman of the Banu Amir was in the sultan's court and heard what had been said. He hastened to the *sayyid* to warn him of the threat to Majnun's life, but Majnun had again fled into the desert. Greatly alarmed, the *sayyid* with his tribesmen searched the wilderness until Majnun was found, in a desolate gorge, writhing like a snake, moaning and sighing, and rising and falling upon the rocks. Tenderly the good *sayyid* gathered his son into his arms, weeping bitterly. So too did Majnun weep. "My father, there is no creature on earth who is not ruled by destiny," he said. "To love Layla is my fate, and never can I throw off my burden. But listen to me, for I have a tale to tell.

Once upon a time, a partridge went hunting in a field and spied an ant, which she seized in her beak by one of its legs. The ant laughed and said, 'You are a skillful hunter, partridge, yet it is a pity that you cannot laugh as I do!' Whereupon the partridge opened her beak to laugh, and the ant escaped. Then the partridge saw how foolish she had been. So it is with man, for he will regret his laughter with bitter tears. Yet I will have nothing to regret, for I have no cause to laugh." And Majnun wept and called out Layla's name.

Then Majnun was carried from the rocky gorge to his own tent, and his kinswomen brought food and water, and his mother whispered many soothing words. But Majnun, staring blankly into the cool darkness of the tent, did not even know her. Several days passed, and when he could rest no longer, he tore open the curtain of his tent and fled again into the desert of the Najd; he roamed under the blistering sun until his face was black and his feet bled from the thorns

Detail from MINIATURE 5

and rocks. "Let Layla's father threaten, for I fear him not! What lover fears a sword?" he asked. "He who goes in search of his beloved cares not for his life!"

So Majnun sang his songs, and from villages and towns both near and far the people came to hear him. They copied down the words, even as they were moved to tears, and carried the poems away with them. And when they knew love themselves, it was with Majnun's words that they sang of the stirrings and the passion of their hearts, for Majnun spoke for lovers everywhere.

Meanwhile, Layla grew more and more beautiful. Indeed, she was the most beautiful maiden in all Arabia. But every day she grew more sorrowful, for from that evening when she had seen Majnun in the moonlight, she had never ceased to love him. From sunrise until sunset, she secretly whispered his name, and in the darkness of night, weeping and sighing, she would go to the door of her tent and listen for his step and watch for his shadow. But she heard only the desert wind, stirring the sand and leaves of the distant trees. She did not have to wait long before she heard his love poems, for they were on the lips of every child in the bazaars and every traveler in the desert. By day, she would repeat them to herself; then, in the secrecy of night, she would fashion songs in response. And indeed, her songs were no less eloquent than Majnun's, for as true as Majnun's was her love. She wrote her songs on scraps of paper, and strew them on the sand; the wind carried them into the villages. Thus did people come upon them, as one stumbles on a precious jewel, and sing them. Soon the songs reached Majnun's ears, and he would sing a reply. As their words were carried back and forth across the desert, so did Layla and Majnun promise one another their undying love.

Now there was a palm grove a short distance from Layla's tent, and every day Layla would go there with her companions. One afternoon, while her friends played among the trees and danced on the green grass which spread around them like an emerald carpet, Layla sat apart, thinking of Majnun and weeping with longing. Suddenly she heard a voice singing loudly outside the garden walls. "How can it be," the voice rang out, "that Layla can dance joyfully in her garden, while her beloved wanders in the wilderness alone?"

When Layla heard this reproach, she wept so bitterly and so mournfully spoke Majnun's name, that none who saw her, not even the most obdurate stone, could remain unmoved. Indeed, one of her companions happened to hear the song, and came upon the weeping Layla; tears of pity filled her eyes. She went to Layla's mother and told what she had heard and seen. Thus did the good woman learn of her daughter's suffering, for never had Layla spoken a word to her about it.

That very day, as it happened, a young man of the tribe of Assad was journeying across the desert and passed by the grove. This Ibn Salam, for such was the young man's name, happened to catch a glimpse of Layla through a chink in the garden wall and immediately fell in love with her. Now Ibn Salam was of a rich and noble family, and he went at once before the chieftain to ask for Layla's hand. The chieftain was well pleased and readily agreed, but asked only that the youth curb his eagerness. "Be patient for a while, my friend," he said. "In but a few months more the bud will blossom into a full-blown rose; then shall the wedding feast be set."

Meanwhile, Majnun still wandered in the desert, dressed in his rags, singing his songs, and crying "Layla! Layla!" He took shelter among some rocks in a gorge where wild animals lived. And one day, a Bedouin prince named Nowfal came upon the gorge and the unhappy Majnun. When he asked his attendants who the mournful creature was, they told of Majnun's suffering. The prince was deeply moved, for while he was brave in battle, he was gentle and kind of heart. Thus he caused a banquet to be set before Majnun. But Majnun would eat no food and drink no wine, and he uttered no word but "Layla!" Then the good prince took his hand and gently said, "My friend, listen to me, for I have heard your story and I wish only to help you. Trust me, and you shall find Layla and shall have her for your own, to love all of your life. Indeed, you shall have Layla, even if I must do battle!"

At these kind words, Majnun arose and embraced Nowfal and went with him to his camp. Under the prince's gracious influence, Majnun became the cheerful youth he had once been. He wore fine robes and a silk turban. Every morning, as the sky brightened with the first rays of the sun, he rode into the wilderness with Nowfal, and they would ride all day. Every evening, when darkness fell, he feasted with the prince and called for wine and listened to the songs of minstrels. Happy were these days, when Majnun's sorrow was allayed. When he looked upon his friend, none was more joyful than Nowfal.

Thus did several months pass, until, one afternoon, the two friends sat together in the shade of a tree, resting from their ride. Majnun sighed bitterly and said, "Good prince, my patience has come to its end. I beg of you, help me find Layla as you promised, for if I must wait even a moment longer, surely I shall die." So mournful did he look that Nowfal leaped to his feet at once, took up his sword, and summoned his men to arms. The next day, at dawn, he rode across the desert with Majnun at his side. When they reached the pasturelands of Layla's tribe and saw the tents on the horizon, they pitched camp. Then Nowfal sent a messenger to Layla's father. "Tell the chieftain that you come to him in Majnun's name and that Majnun must have Layla. Tell him, too, that if he should refuse, in Majnun's name will I attack!"

When the chieftain heard this threat, he was enraged. "Rather than give my daughter to this madman, I will fight like a lion and even die!"

Then Nowfal sent an even stronger threat to the chieftain, and with many curses the chieftain refused. So Nowfal set upon Layla's people, and the desert resounded with the clash of war. In the midst of the fighting, Majnun huddled and wept and prayed for peace. He could not fight, for every injury to Layla's tribesmen was as a wound to him. Indeed, he would have drawn his bow and arrow against his own army had not shame stayed his hand. At last, as the sun descended in all its crimson glory, a truce was called and both armies retreated to their camps. Nowfal again sent a messenger to the chieftain, offering many jewels and precious gifts in return for Layla, the most precious jewel of all. The chieftain scornfully refused. His army greatly outnumbered Nowfal's, for he had summoned many tribesmen from surrounding pastures and hunting grounds. But the next morning Nowfal left his camp and went to amass an even greater force, enlisting tribesmen from Medina all the way to Baghdad, and the fighting began anew. At dawn one day Nowfal attacked; by dusk the chieftain was defeated and knelt at Nowfal's feet. "I am a weak old man," he said. "I have no strength; my men are all dispersed. Do what you will with me, but there is only one thing I ask. Give Layla not to Majnun, for he is a fool and has disgraced his name and hers!"

Now Nowfal, as we have said, was gentle of heart, and when the chieftain spoke, tears of compassion rose to the prince's eyes. Had not Nowfal gone to battle for the sake of Majnun? And had not Majnun kissed the bodies of Layla's kinsmen as they fell dead? Was Majnun not a traitor as well as a madman? Thus, with a heavy sigh, Nowfal agreed to the chieftain's request and bid him farewell. Then he gave the order to break camp. Whereupon Majnun turned to the prince and spoke many bitter words; he then took his few possessions and rode off into the desert. Trembling with rage and weeping with despair, he cried out "Layla! Layla!" And his cries echoed across the dunes. Greatly alarmed, Nowfal went in search of Majnun the next morning, but he was nowhere to be found, and Nowfal saw him not that day, or the day after, or ever again.

For many days Majnun rode deep into the desert; he saw not a living soul, only stones and thorn-bushes and miles of sand. Suddenly he came upon two gazelles caught in a trap. A hunter was standing over them with his dagger raised. When Majnun looked into the gentle eyes of the gazelles he remembered Layla's soft black eyes, and he cried, "I beg of you, good hunter, do not kill!"

"Indeed, I am a poor man with a wife and family to feed," the hunter said. "For two months have I waited for this catch. What will you give me in exchange for the gazelles?"

Whereupon Majnun dismounted from his horse and placed the reins in the hunter's hands. The hunter rode off. Majnun freed the gazelles, and they ran gracefully away. Now Majnun walked in the desert. Thorns tore at his robes and scratched his feet, but he noticed not as he stumbled through the hot sand calling out Layla's name.

The next day Majnun came upon a stag caught in a net and wounded in the neck. Standing over the stag was a hunter with his knife drawn. "I beg of you, good hunter, release this stag at once!" cried Majnun. "Do you not think of the pain of those whose suffering you cause?"

"I do not wish to kill the stag," the hunter said, "but how will I survive? What will you give me if I let the stag go free?" Whereupon Majnun gave to the hunter all that remained of his possessions, and the hunter went off. Then Majnun freed the stag and watched it make its way across the sand. Majnun continued walking in the desert calling out Layla's name.

On the third day, the sun glared down so fiercely that the sand seemed to shimmer, and Majnun sat in the shade of a date-palm tree. Now on a branch of the tree there sat a crow, and Majnun spoke to the bird. "Why are you dressed in black? Do you share my sorrow, that your feathers are as black as Layla's hair? If you do mourn, like me, why don't you leave me." The crow did not answer, but hopped onto another branch, then flew away into the stifling air. And so Majnun sat alone all day, until the sun set and the sky turned red, then blue, till it became blacker even than the feathers of the crow.

Then Majnun slept, and at the dawn, when he awoke, he saw an old woman dragging by a rope an old man whose legs and arms were bound with chains. When the old woman came near, Majnun asked her who she was and why the old man was in chains. She replied that she was a widow and he was a dervish and that they traveled through the desert in this way and begged for food and shared what scraps were thrown to them. Then Majnun fell to his knees. "It is I who should be in chains, not he!" he cried. "Free this man, and put this rope around my neck instead, and you shall have all of our food!"

The woman agreed, and she led Majnun through the wilderness. Whenever they came to a village, or even a shepherd's hut, Majnun would sing his songs and dance and hit his head upon the ground and cry out "Layla! Layla!" and they would be given scraps of food. Thus they wandered through the desert until, one day, they happened upon a camp. Majnun saw Layla's tent. He hit his head against a rock; tears streamed from his eyes, and he cried, "Layla! Layla! I have caused your people to suffer at the hands of Nowfal. As punishment I am in chains. Behold me and my grief!" And, with a howl, he tore his chains apart and flung them from him. Then he cast away the rope and fled into the mountains.

Now it happened that after Nowfal's victory, the chieftain had told Layla of Nowfal's agreement. Layla had listened in silence and then had gone to her tent and wept, for never, not even for a moment, had her love for Majnun faltered. Soon after that, Ibn Salam came back to claim Layla as his bride. He came with many caravans laden with gifts and showered silks and gold upon the chieftain. Carpets were spread, and a wedding feast was set. For seven days and seven nights, and for seven days more, there was great celebration: fires were lit; incense of aloe was burned; silver coins were thrown into the air. Then, the next morning, when barely had the stars yielded to the rising sun, Ibn Salam departed with his bride. When the caravan reached the lands of the tribe of Assad, the joyful bridegroom said to Layla, "Everything you see is yours, my love!"

But that night, when he went to embrace her, Layla withdrew. When he still would take her in his arms, she struck him. "Come not within arm's length of me," she said, "for I have vowed never to give myself to you. Take your sword and kill me if you will, but I will not submit, not even in a hundred years!" So great was Ibn Salam's love for Layla, that he fell to his knees and asked her forgiveness, gently saying, "Rather would I be allowed to look upon your face than lose you forever." And thus did they live and so a year passed.

During that year Majnun wandered in the wilderness. One day, while he was lying in the sand exhausted, a stranger, a black-skinned man, passed by. Now he knew well who Majnun was and said to him, "Have you not heard? Layla is married! Her husband is rich and noble, and even this very moment does he hold her in his arms! Better to turn your back on Layla than to scorn the world, my friend!"

At these words, Majnun moaned with despair and fainted. When he at last opened his eyes, the stranger was overcome with pity. "My friend, forgive me, for I have been wicked and have spoken falsely. Layla is married, yet she loves you still and shares not her husband's bed. She is chaste and longs for you with all her heart and soul!"

Then the stranger departed, and Majnun stumbled through the desert, weeping and shaking to the depths of his being. In one breath, he called out Layla's name and sang his songs; in the next, he reproached her for betraying him; then he wept and cried out his forgiveness.

Now in all this time, the good *sayyid* grew weak with age. He grieved greatly for his son and resolved to go once more into the desert to find him. Taking a walking stick, he set out with two companions. After journeying for many days, he came upon a desolate cave where he found Majnun, wasted and drawn. When Majnun heard his father's voice, he wept. Then the *sayyid* said, "I beg of you, my son, come home, for I am close to death. When I die, I wish to have you at my side."

Detail from MINIATURE 5

But Majnun shook his head; he heard his father's words but understood them not, for he knew only that he loved, not who he was or what was his name. And, weeping, he replied, "My father, I am lost to you and can never return. I live like the wild animals that roam around me; I am a stranger to my tribe." With sorrow in his heart, the *sayyid* saw that this was so. He left Majnun in his forsaken cave and returned to the camp of the Banu Amir, and shortly thereafter he died.

One day, while hunting in the desert, a kinsman came upon Majnun and told him of his father's death and spoke many bitter words. "Wicked son of a good father, may you pray for forgiveness for your sins!" At this doleful news Majnun wept; he went at once to his father's grave, and prayed for a day and a night for forgiveness. Then he went back into the wilderness.

When he returned to the cave, the animals of the desert came to his side. First the lion, then the very stag that he had saved, and then the antelope, and the wolf, and the fox; the wild ass joined their company, and the hare, and the timid gazelle. Majnun ruled over them all; a king was he, and his cave was his court. All around were rocks and thorns and burning sand. No place on earth was more desolate than this, yet Majnun called it paradise, for here he lived in peace with all his friends. Among the animals there was perfect harmony; the lion lay with the lamb; the wolf chased not the hare; the gazelle went undisturbed before the fox.

Every day, Majnun and his animals wandered in the wilderness and dug among the stones for roots and herbs. As the sun descended, they would feast together. Majnun would speak of Layla and sing his songs, and the beasts would listen quietly and sadly bow their heads. Then darkness fell. Majnun lay down to sleep; with his great bushy tail the fox swept clean Majnun's resting place. The wild ass was Majnun's pillow; his knees rested on the haunches of the antelope, and the gazelle caressed his feet. Throughout the night, until the break of dawn, the wolf kept watch.

For many hours at a time, Majnun would gaze fondly on his animals, and he was wont to say, "Now that I am among my friends, surely I am the happiest man of all!" And he would think upon a story he had heard, years before, of a young courtier at the palace of the king of Merv. This king kept a pack of ferocious dogs, and it was his wont, whenever anyone displeased him, to throw that person to the dogs to be devoured. When the youth heard the dogs' barking and the victims' cries and moans, he resolved to cultivate the friendship of the keeper of the dogs, and then he won the friendship of the dogs themselves. One day, the courtier aroused the king's anger, and the king ordered him thrown to the dogs. But the dogs would not harm the youth, for he was their friend. When the king saw this, he tamed the beast of his own soul.

So did the wild animals guard Majnun against harm. After some time, two visitors came into the wilderness and approached the cave. The first was an old man; he had flowing white hair and a face so kind and gentle that the lion's growling ceased and the wolf showed not his teeth. They let the old man pass. Majnun greeted him and asked, "My friend, what good news do you bring?"

Whereupon the old man brought forth a letter. Majnun seized it eagerly. "Know that I have seen Layla," the old man said. "One day I came upon her grieving in a garden; so great was her sorrow that I bade her speak. She wept and said, 'A thousand times madder am I than Majnun, for he is free to wander where he pleases, while I am but a prisoner in my camp. A thousand times greater than Majnun's are my torments. Though I cannot be with him, I hunger for news of him. Where does he go? What does he say? Has he companions? I beg of you, search for him until you find him, and tell me how he is!' Indeed, these are her very words. When I promised to search for you, she wrote this letter and gave it to me to give to you."

Then Majnun read Layla's letter; his heart quickened with joy, for all that the old man said was true. At once, he asked the old man for a paper and pen, and he wrote a reply. "I beg of you, take this to Layla, with my love!" he cried. And the old man rode into the desert, to Layla's camp, and brought the letter to her.

Now the second visitor to the cave was Majnun's uncle Salim Amiri. He came into the desert bringing food and clothing. Majnun was glad to see him, for his uncle was a good man and as a boy Majnun had loved him dearly. He put on the robes but gave the food to the wild beasts. When he did this his uncle sighed and said, "Listen to me, for I have a story to tell.

Once upon a time, in this very land of Arabia, a king was riding in this very desert, and he happened to pass a hut. He learned that in this miserable dwelling there lived a dervish who hardly ate and never slept, and he sent an attendant to speak to the dervish. The dervish said that he ate only herbs gathered from the fields. 'Indeed, you should have far better food if you were in the service of the king,' said the attendant, but the dervish shook his head. When the king heard of this, he said, 'The dervish is a wise man, and he is superior even to me. He knows well the worth of what he has and is satisfied.' Then the king went into the hut and kissed the dervish's feet."

When Salim Amiri had finished his tale, he said that he would bring Majnun's mother to the desert, for she had grown old and greatly longed to see her son. When the good woman was brought to the cave, she wept and washed the dust from Majnun's body and plucked the thorns from his feet. All the while she pleaded with him to return to his people, but to no avail. "The Banu Amir are your people; they are mine no longer," Majnun said. "I know only the desert and my animals." Bent with sorrow, the old woman returned to her tribe. Shortly thereafter, she breathed her last. Then Salim Amiri again visited Majnun, and told him of his mother's death. Majnun went to her tomb and mourned and wept. There he met some of his kinsmen, and they spoke bitterly to him and reproached him angrily. After a day and a night, he again fled to the desert.

All this time Layla waited eagerly for an answer to her letter. Every night she slipped from her tent and stood at the crossroads of her village, watching and listening for the old man. At last, one night, he came and gave her Majnun's letter. When she read it, she rewarded the good man with jewels and a sack of coins and asked him to bring Majnun to a grove nearby. "The trees grow as thickly as a wall, so we shall not be seen. Tell my beloved that Layla longs to hear him sing his songs!"

And so it was that one night the old man led Majnun into the grove. The faithful animals followed and stood patiently outside. The old man brought Layla into the grove. She stayed at a distance from Majnun, for like a moth fatally drawn to a flame, she feared that she would perish. Instead she sat beneath a tree and listened, but heard not a sound, for Majnun had fainted. The old man revived him, and then he sang the most beautiful love poem he had ever composed. Then the lovers gazed upon each other with joy and wonder, as they had when they were children. But all too soon the moment passed; Majnun fled, and Layla went back to her tent.

When Majnun returned to his desolate cave, a young man came to him. Now this youth, whose name was Salam Baghdadi, begged Majnun to teach him his songs and poems. He stayed with Majnun in the desert and learned them all. Then he went to Baghdad and many other villages and cities and sang Majnun's words wherever he went, that all who loved might hear.

Soon after, Ibn Salam was taken ill with a fever as violent as the desert wind, and in a few days he was dead. At last Layla could weep without restraint, for all who looked upon her thought that she wept for her young husband, and they pitied her with all their hearts. Yet for Majnun only did she mourn. Now in Arabia it was the custom for a widow to seclude herself in her tent for two years, speaking to no one. Layla went dutifully to her tent; she welcomed the solitude and vowed that every moment she would think of Majnun.

This ritual she performed until autumn, when the trees blazed with color and the wind rose. During her many months of solitude Layla became so weak that she could no longer rise from her bed. Her weakness turned to fever, and she called her mother to her and told her what the good woman had known for many years. "Grant me one wish, my mother," Layla said. "When I die, for I am like an autumn leaf on the branches of the tree of life, I will be dressed in bridal robes. Thus shall I wait for my beloved, for surely Majnun will come to my grave. And I would have you comfort him as you would comfort me."

The next day, as the scarlet leaves fluttered to the ground, Layla died, and her mother did as she had promised. When Majnun heard of Layla's death, he went at once to her grave and wept from the depths of his soul. Indeed, he wept his heart's blood, and some say that as he wept, the flowers that grew at Layla's grave turned red. He sang his songs and again likened Layla to the graceful gazelle. For a month did Majnun stay at Layla's grave, guarded by his animals. As time passed he grew weaker and weaker. It was in a voice barely a whisper that he prayed to God to release him from his earthly form and bring him to Layla's side. Soon after his prayers were answered; his animals guarded his body with fierce growls, so that none could touch him. Only when he crumbled into dust did the animals go back to the wilderness. Then Majnun's tribesmen came forth and gathered his bones and buried them by Layla's side. All that day, and for many days after, there was mourning in the camp of the Banu Amir and in the camp of Layla's people.

For many years the story of Layla and Majnun has been told and told again, for never did there live two lovers as true as they.

COMMENTARY

Layla and Majnun

"Layla and Majnun" is perhaps the most popular romance in the Islamic world. Versions appear in prose, song, and poetry in almost every language within the vast area stretching from the Atlantic Ocean to the Chinese border. But because of the psychological depth and universality invested in the story, Nizami's epic still serves as the model for all others.

The poem was commissioned by Shirvanshah Akhsetan, a Caucasian ruler proud of his Iranian origin and a benefactor of Persian culture. In the preface of "Layla and Majnun," Nizami explains that one beautiful day, while he was perusing a collection of his own poetry in his garden, a messenger from Shirvanshah arrived and presented to him a letter in the ruler's hand. Describing Nizami as "the universal magician of eloquence,"[1] Shirvanshah asked the poet to create a romance based not on a Persian epic, but on a simple Arab folktale, the story of Majnun, the love-mad poet, and Layla, the sequestered beauty.

For centuries, this legend had been a popular theme of the short love sonnets and songs of the Bedouins who lived in the Arabian peninsular, and during the early days of the Muslim era, it had been absorbed and embellished by the Persians. Majnun is traditionally identified with a poet known as Qays ibn al-Mulawwah, who probably lived in the second half of the seventh century A.D. in the Najd desert of Arabia. One of the earlier written accounts of the Majnun story is presented in the *Treatise on Poetry and Poets* by Ibn Qutayba, who died in 275 A.H./899 A.D.[2] In the *Anthology of Poetry*, written by Ibn Dawud,[3] a close contemporary of Ibn Qutayba, there are poetic passages ascribed to Majnun. In the comprehensive collection of literary records known as the *Books of Songs,* compiled by Abu al-Faraj al-Isfahani[4] in the tenth century, there are also many poems and anecdotes attributed to Majnun. Although it is probable that there was more than one love-crazed poet called Majnun—that is, "possessed by a jinn or a genie; a madman"—in 1946 the Russian scholar Krachkovski erased most doubts as to his historical identity.[5]

Neither the arid desert setting nor the spare plot of Majnun and Layla's romance inspired Nizami's poetic vision. The story, he commented, offered "neither gardens nor royal festivities, neither streams nor wines nor happiness. In the arid sands and rugged mountains, the poetry sinks into grief."[6] But Nizami could not refuse the royal commission; furthermore, his dearly beloved son Muhammad urged him to accept it. And so he expanded and deepened the plot and the personalities, creating from the fragmentary versions a full-scale dramatic poem.

For his romance, Nizami chose an easy meter, the short *Hazaj mussadas* which scans as follows:
/ − − ◡ / ◡ − ◡ − / ◡ − − // − − ◡ / ◡ − ◡ − / ◡ − − /
Hazaj means trilling of a singer, a twanging, joyful sound in which Arabic and Persian poems are often sung; *mussadas* means composed of six feet. Nizami found in this easy, straight, and happy meter a counterbalance to the gloom of the story and the aridity of the desert environment. He also sought to enliven the desert setting with rhapsodic descriptions of nature—its dawns, dusks, and skies filled with glittering stars. As in his other poems, he allegorized the changing seasons to enrich its background.

"Layla and Majnun" is comprised of at least 4,000 distichs. Nizami wrote that it took "less than four months" to compose and that if he had had nothing else to do he would have finished it in an even shorter period of time.[7] This implies a trance-like state of writing, for it averages to at least 1,000 distichs or 2,000 lines per month. It probably did not include the thorough research Nizami undertook in order to develop background material for the poem.

The exact number of distichs has long been a source of scholarly fascination and controversy, especially since those that are considered apocryphal alter the plot significantly. Vahid Dastgerdi's critical edition, based on thirty manuscripts copied between the fourteenth and seventeenth centuries, totals 4,650 distichs. Dastgerdi considers 600 of these to be spurious, added by later writers and scribes who also transposed an additional 400 distichs to cover their handiwork. R. Gelpke considers Dastgerdi's the only authoritative text and based his prose adaptation of "Layla and Majnun" upon it.[8]

E. G. Browne, H. Massé, and A. J. Arberry, however, have translated many passages as authentic which Dastgerdi and Gelpke consider interpolations. E. É. Bertels, the Russian editor of the Persian text published in 1965, found 4,659 distichs valid, using the ten most famous manuscripts—the earliest dating from the fourteenth century. They are in the collections of the Bibliothèque Nationale, Paris; the British Museum, London; the Bodleian Library, Oxford; and in collections in libraries and museums in the Soviet Union. It is, of course, possible that Nizami himself rewrote the poem, making his own changes and additions. Many of the great poets who imitated Nizami included so-called spurious passages and plots, and their poetic sensibility should be respected.

Some manuscripts of "Layla and Majnun" bear the date 584 A.H./1188 A.D. as the year it was completed; others, 588 A.H./1192 A.D.; still others, as was common in copied manuscripts, give both dates. The earlier year is supported in the text by *abjad,* the Arabic alphabetical system which assigns numerical values to letters. In the course of the poem, Nizami tells us that he is forty-nine years old, but as his birth year is disputed, this information does not help in setting the date of the poem.

Whatever its length and its exact date of completion, there is no doubt that Nizami used all the material, written and oral, available to him, adding, altering, and transforming as his poetic genius prompted, in order to create this tragic masterpiece. He brought together in splendid tension the sparsensess of the Arabian desert and the opulence of the Persian garden. As R. Gelpke states:

"Nizami preserves the Bedouin atmosphere, the nomads' tents in the desert and the tribal customs of the inhabitants, while at the same time transposing the story into the far more civilized Iranian world.... Majnun talks to the planets in the symbolic language of a twelfth-century Persian sage, the encounters of small Arabic raiding parties become gigantic battles of royal Persian armies and most of the Bedouins talk like the heroes, courtiers, and savants of the refined Iranian civilizations."[9]

Nizami's originality, however, lies not so much in these brilliant scenic descriptions, but rather in his psychological portrayal of the richness and complexity of the human soul when confronted with intense and abiding love. Majnun's compulsions, anxieties, frustrations, and passions are not slighted as he moves inexorably toward an ideal love that involves renunciation and, ultimately, transcendence.

Even at its most blissful, love is accompanied by pain which separation only intensifies. "Yet do not think," Nizami says, "that such a pain is to be deplored, for it rewards the person by relieving him of himself. Having killed the self, the lover becomes identified with the beloved."[10] Many critics have interpreted this as mystical love. But if there is a mystic strain in Nizami, it is subtle and covert; it never destroys or blurs the sharp psychological and the physical identity of its protagonist. It is virtually impossible to draw a clear line in "Layla and Majnun," or in any of Nizami's poetry, between the mystical and the erotic, the sacred and the profane.

The psychological profile of Layla is less deeply drawn, but her enduring love is no less extraordinary an achievement. Although she reluctantly defers to the will of her family and her tribe and marries another, she will not share his bed. Dying, she asks to be dressed as a bride, to be joined in purest ecstasy with her beloved Majnun.

Nevertheless, true to his need to present all facets of human experience in his tales, Nizami included these observations in the romance:

Woman does not keep her promise—not even one in a thousand.
Woman does only what satisfies her.
Woman is faithless from beginning to end.
Woman loves you—until the next man appears on the horizon.

Woman is more lustful and passionate than man.
Woman is not trustworthy.
Woman is a cheat.
Woman is deceitful.
Woman is perverse.
Woman causes sufferance; fidelity is not her game.
Woman is peace on the surface; she is turmoil within.
Woman's enmity is destructive.
Woman's friendship corrupts.
Woman's qualities are too numerous to count.[11]

In the story of "Khosrow and Shirin," after many misfortunes caused by inner and outer forces, the lovers are finally united and spend several happy years together before their deaths. In contrast, Layla and Majnun are scourged by separation, social ostracism, self-denial, and spiritual and physical suffering from the very beginning until their tragic ends. It is quite possible that, to soften the tragedy, Nizami wrote a second version, weaving into it the love story of Zayd for his cousin Zaynab, which parallels that of Majnun and Layla. The couples become messengers for one another and to some degree are able to mitigate the relentless curse of separation. But Layla and Majnun's love remains unconsummated; Majnun cannot bear physical duality, declaring that he already carries Layla spiritually within his soul. His fate is unyielding and, to a large extent, self-imposed. In a popular Arabic saying, Majnun declares: "From the time Layla was a little girl and her breast had not yet developed, I loved her. We were two little children looking after grazing sheep. I wish we had never grown up, nor had the sheep."

The expanded version of "Layla and Majnun" closes with a vivid dream sequence, replete with nightingales, golden fruit, perfumed flowers, and crystal streams. Majnun and Layla, sitting on magnificent carpets, are radiantly embracing, wine cups in hand. Many scholars believe this to be an interpolation, but if its date can be drawn from the moving dedication to Shirvanshah's crown prince, in which Nizami counsels his son Muhammad whom he addresses as a boy of fourteen, the entire Zayd–Zaynab addition may well be Nizami's own work. The opportunities it offers for love's consummation certainly heighten the drama and the poignancy of its renunciation.

Imitators of Nizami's "Layla and Majnun" can be listed by the hundreds, and the romance is popular even today. According to E. É. Bertels and A. Hikmat, counting only the most famous versions, there are twenty in Persian, forty in Turkish, three in Azarbaijani, one in Uzbek, one in Kurdish, and two in Tajik. It is truly a treasury of the human spirit. As the Turkish poet Hamdi wrote at the end of the fifteenth century, in the introduction to his rendering of "Layla and Majnun": "'Layla and Majnun' is the furnace of love's fire, yet it is the rose garden of the soul."[12]

1. Vahid Dastgerdi, critical edition of "Layla and Majnun" (Teheran, 1313 A.H./1933 A.D.; reprinted 1333 A.H./1954 A.D.), p. 25.
2. Ibn Qutayba, *Kitab al-Shi'r wa al-Shu'ara* (Beirut, 1964).
3. Ibn Dawud, *Kitab al-Zahra (The Book of the Flower)* (Chicago, 1932).
4. Abu al-Faraj al-Isfahani, *Kitab al-Aghani* (Beirut, 1955).
5. I. Y. Krachkovski, "Die Frühgeschichte der Erzählung von Macnun und Laila in der Arabischen Literatur," translated by H. Ritter, *Oriens*, 1955, vol. 8, no. 1, pp. 1–50.
6. V. Dastgerdi, op. cit., p. 25.
7. Ibid., p. 29.
8. Nizami, *The Story of Layla and Majnun,* translated from the Persian and edited by R. Gelpke (London, 1966), p. 220.
9. Ibid., p. 218.
10. Dastgerdi, op. cit., p. 84.
11. Ibid., p. 151.
12. E. J. Gibb, *A History of Ottoman Poetry* (London, 1965), vol. 2, p. 175.

The Seven Princesses

In days of old, when Yazdegerd was king of all Persia, the land flourished as never before. Heroes performed brave deeds, and poets were inspired to sing great songs; palaces of unsurpassing splendor raised their domes against the sky. Harvests were plentiful, the markets bustled, and the wealth of the kingdom mounted like dunes of drifting desert sand.

Now in this glorious time the king had all he could desire but one thing—a son to sit beside him and inherit his throne. Years passed and still there was no child; dark grew Yazdegerd's forebodings. Then at last a son was born, and he was named Bahram. At the very moment of Bahram's birth, the royal astrologers searched their charts. They traced the rise and fall of every star, and when they finished their calculations, they went before the king. "Magnificence," the eldest said, "your son will have good fortune; all the stars concur. But if he is to fulfill his happy future, he must be raised among the Arabs in a far-off land."

And so it was that Bahram grew to manhood in the court of Yemen, in a residence built for him. He was schooled in mathematics and astronomy, riding and polo, and the art of war. He excelled in all he did; but more than anything the prince enjoyed the hunt. So skilled was he with the bow and arrow that he soon became a legend throughout Arabia.

One day, while Bahram was hunting, he came upon a lion tearing the back and neck of a wild ass. As the two beasts struggled, the young prince drew his bow, and with unerring aim he launched an arrow. The arrow passed through the shoulders of the lion and the ass, and pinned them both together to the ground. When Bahram's companions saw what he had done, so great was their amazement that they called him Bahram Gur—*gur* being the word for "wild ass." Moreover, the king of Yemen ordered the feat celebrated in murals on the walls of Bahram's residence. So skillfully were the lion and the wild ass drawn, that all who saw the paintings thought they were real.

Now the residence of Bahram Gur was curious, for it had been built by a magician, and not the least of all its curiosities was a door that was always locked. One day, by chance, the prince came upon this door, and, unable to open it, bid his chamberlain unlock it. Obediently the servant took his key and undid the lock and led the prince across the threshold. The room Bahram Gur entered was a treasure-house of dazzling splendor, such as had never been seen before. On the walls were seven portraits of seven princesses from seven different regions of the earth. Dark and fair, slender and full, sober and smiling, their beauty was so perfect as to make diamonds seem dim, rubies drab, and emeralds as cheap as dross. By each of these lovely portraits was the prince's heart captured. And then, to his amazement, he came upon a likeness of himself, and beneath the likeness was an inscription saying that he would wed all seven princesses, once he became king; so much was ordained by the stars. The inscription filled him with joy, and he went often to the room to contemplate the portraits, and to savor his future happiness.

Meanwhile, word of his prowess reached the court of Persia. King Yazdegerd, now weak with age, was afraid. He feared that if Bahram Gur were king he would favor the Arabs over the Persians, and so Yazdegerd declined to appoint his son as heir. When at last the good king died, the Persian nobles placed upon the throne a ruler of their choice. When Bahram Gur learned of his father's death and of the usurpation of his rightful place, he was greatly angered. To determine who should be the ruler of all Persia, he proposed a contest. The crown of Persia would be set between two lions. He who could, bare-handed, wrest it from their claws, should place it on his head. Urged by his elders, the new king reluctantly agreed, and, like a moon between the jaws of two fierce dragons, the crown was placed between the beasts. Bahram Gur strode fearlessly between the lions; he shouted so mightily that their roaring was but a whisper, and with his hands he killed the beasts, seized the crown, and fixed it upon his head. Thus did the glorious reign of Bahram Gur begin.

Throughout the land of Persia there was great rejoicing, and the people crowded at the palace gates. Bahram Gur went before them, and promised to rule with justice, to free them from the burden of taxes for seven years, and to open the royal granaries to all in times of drought. And so the kingdom prospered as in the days of Yazdegerd. With the people now happy, Bahram Gur was able to attend to his own pleasures. He hunted in the desert and enjoyed the company of beautiful women. And the one who pleased him most was Fetneh the musician. Often, when he rode to the hunt, she would ride with him, and as he searched for game she would play sweetly on her harp.

One day, when they had ridden to the desert and the king had killed many wild asses, Fetneh failed to praise him for his skill. Incensed, Bahram Gur asked how she would have him make the kill. Fetneh, who had mischief in her heart, replied that he should pin its hoof to its ear. Whereupon the king found an ass, shot an arrow and grazed its ear. As the ass raised its hoof to rub the scratch, Bahram Gur let fly a second arrow, and pinned the hoof to the ear. Yet even then Fetneh failed to praise his skill. "You do this through practice," she taunted. "In everything, my king, practice makes perfect." Thus the king's anger turned to rage, and he ordered her put to death.

Now Fetneh repented of her mockery, and knew that in a few days' time the king's fury would cease. She begged her guard to spare her for a week. The guard was to go to Bahram Gur and tell him that Fetneh was dead; if the king rejoiced, she should be put to death at once, but if he grieved, she should be spared. The guard, fearing for his life if he obeyed the king's order and thus displeased him, agreed. And so, after seven days, he went to Bahram Gur, and told him that Fetneh was dead. Tears flowed from Bahram's eyes. And Fetneh was spared. The guard then sent her to his own country residence, far from the court.

Now the guard's house had a pavilion that was reached by sixty stairs, and soon after Fetneh arrived a calf was born, and Fetneh climbed to the pavilion carrying the newborn calf. And every day for six years she climbed to the pavilion with her burden. And the calf grew into an ox, and she could still carry it with ease. Then she asked the faithful guard to invite the king to visit his country residence and share a feast.

So it happened that one day Bahram Gur was hunting on the plain nearby, and saw the high pavilion. He asked his company whose residence it was, and the guard came forth. The house was his, he told the king, and asked him to be his guest. When Bahram Gur arrived, everything was in readiness to receive and honor him; carpets were spread beneath the hooves of his horse, and jewels were scattered on his head. Then they climbed the sixty stairs to the pavilion, where a magnificent feast was set. "Tell me, my friend," Bahram Gur asked his host, "how will you climb these sixty stairs when you have reached the age of sixty years?"

The guard replied that at the age of sixty he would climb the stairs with ease. Indeed, he said, there was a woman in his household who carried an ox up those sixty stairs each day as if it were a feather. The king demanded that he see this done at once. And so Fetneh, first covering her face with a veil, took the ox, and carried it up the sixty stairs to the pavilion and placed it as a gift at the king's feet. Then she asked Bahram Gur how he supposed she had been able to perform this feat, and he replied that the secret must be practice. "You see, my king, in everything, practice makes perfect," said Fetneh, lowering her veil. And when the king saw who she was, he cried aloud with joy.

Now in all this time, as Bahram Gur pursued his pleasures, he attended less and less to his royal duties. The kingdom weakened with neglect, and it was not long before word of Persia's sorry state reached the court of China. The Chinese emperor, greedy for conquest, plotted an attack. In his scheme he was aided by certain Persian nobles who had grown disenchanted with their king and had sent secret messages to China. As the secret messages went back and forth, the emperor's forces gathered. Bahram Gur knew well what was afoot, yet feigned ignorance, until suddenly one night he summoned his army, attacked the emperor's camp, and drove the invaders back across the river Oxus. Then he rebuked his faithless nobles for their treachery, and announced to them that the drinking of wine only increased his power, though it sapped the strength of ordinary men. The chastened nobles then spoke in praise of Bahram Gur, and once again the land of Persia flourished, and the king pursued his pleasures.

Often, in this time of peace and plenty, the king would think of the days of his youth in the land of Yemen and remember the locked door and the wonderful room beyond it. He would remember the portraits of the seven beautiful princesses and marvel at the glorious things that were to be. And as time passed, through his wealth and by force, Bahram Gur obtained the hand of each of the seven beautiful princesses. He had only to await their arrival in the land of Persia.

That winter, the king held a great feast. Outside all was cold and bleak, while within all was bright and warm. Fires burned in every hearth, wine flowed, and as the red of the fires mingled with the ruby red of the wine, and with the even deeper red of the rich carpets, the king's musicians played from dusk to dawn. Now during this banquet there came before the king one Shideh, a craftsman of the greatest skill; he had mastered the arts of painting, sculpture, architecture, and calligraphy, and knew as well the principles of mathematics and astronomy. This Shideh proposed to build a palace of unsurpassed magnificence, with seven lofty domes and seven sumptuous pavilions for each of the seven beautiful princesses. Each dome was to be a different color and was to be constructed according to the position, in the sky, of the planet that governed that color. The pavilions, to be the same colors as their domes, were to be furnished with the finest carpets and silk hangings, the most precious metals and woods, the sweetest wines, and the most fragrant flowers that were to be found in all of Persia.

For several days the king pondered this proposal. Then he summoned Shideh and told the craftsman to consult the heavens. At the first auspicious moment, he was to begin his work. After two years of unceasing labor, the residence was completed; such was the king's delight that he showered Shideh with splendid gifts. Then the seven beautiful princesses arrived in Persia, and each was taken to her own pavilion, and Bahram Gur prepared himself for the pleasures that had been foretold.

The Black Pavilion

"Even as the planets move, so then shall I," said Bahram Gur. "I will visit one pavilion a day from the first of the week till the last." Thus, on Saturday, the day of Saturn, Bahram Gur, dressed all in black, entered the black pavilion. The Princess Furak, the youngest daughter of the Indian rajah, awaited him. Sweet was the air with music and the incense of aloes, and lovely was the Indian princess, with her sable skin and agate eyes. All that day, in the darkness of the black pavilion, Bahram Gur enjoyed her charms. At last night fell, and the sky became dark. The birds, mistaking Furak's beauty for the radiance of the dawn, began to sing. But daybreak was still many hours away when the enchanted king made his request. "A story, my love," he murmured. "I would have a story."

And with a languid smile, the princess Furak began her tale.

Once, oh king, a long time ago, there lived a lady of great goodness and beauty. One day a month, every month of the year, she visited our palace. She was always welcome, for no one failed to love her; yet she was strange, for she dressed only in black. From head to foot, dark was she as is the pavilion in which we now lie. When at last she was asked the reason for this mournful custom, her reply was ready. It is her story that I tell you now.

Years before, when she was very young, this lady passed her days and nights as a slave-girl to a king; a king to whom she lost her heart. Now this king was ever carefree and high-spirited; he enjoyed the company of boisterous young men and the favors of beautiful women. In his palace laughter reigned, and wine flowed like a river. No traveler was ever turned away. Whenever a stranger came, a banquet would be set and cupbearers called forth; and after the feast was done, the stranger would be asked to tell his story, for the king was always curious to learn of life. He was a Rainbow King, for his palace shone with all the colors of the world, and his was a Rainbow Court.

Then one day, the colors darkened; the feasting and the revels ceased. The king shut up his palace as if it were a prison and retired from his court as if it had been struck by plague. When at last he showed himself again, his brilliant robes and jewels were gone; from head to foot, he wore only black. His companions tried to cheer him, but nothing could lift the gloom that had settled on his soul. Vainly did they question him, until at last, in words heavy with grief, the king revealed the reason for his woe.

Some time ago, he said, a traveler had come to the palace dressed all in black. The king, as was his wont, had asked the traveler to speak about himself, but the stranger only shook his head. And so the king asked yet again, and many times again until, after a week of coaxing, the traveler fell to his knees. "I beg of you, my king, do not ask the secret of my sorrow. Yet if any man, much less a king, must know, then I cannot refuse. Know, then, that in my youthful days I made my way to China, and in that far-off land I came upon the cause of my despair. Know that there is a place for those who dress only in black, and that this place, my king, is called the City of the Stupified."

Then the stranger paused; more than this he would not tell. When he asked to leave the palace and continue on his way, the king reluctantly agreed. And so the traveler departed. For a long time afterward, the king thought on what the traveler had said. So strange was the story that he could think of little else. Finally, consumed by curiosity, he dispatched his messengers throughout the land to find the traveler, but there was not a trace. And there was none in all the land who knew about the City of the Stupified.

Unsatisfied, the king resolved to journey to the land of China. For many days and many nights did the king travel—over high mountains, across wide rivers, through scorching deserts and forests thick with trees. He paused for not a moment's rest until, finally, one evening, as the sun descended from the sky, he beheld a city rising in the distance, a paradise gleaming in the cool blue dusk. Yet as the king drew near, he saw that this was not a paradise at all, for on rooftop after rooftop there fluttered not banners of rejoicing, but flags of black. And in the streets the citizens wandered back and forth, dressed all in black.

That evening the king found a residence for himself, and settled there and told not who he was. Then did he seek to learn the secret of the city's sorrow. The townspeople would not speak, but every morning they raised their mournful flags. Thus did a whole year pass. Every night the king retired with less hope than he had known that very dawn. At the year's end, it happened that he met a kind and simple man, an honest man, true of heart. He was a butcher, and upon him the king lavished gifts as only kings can bestow: carpets and porcelains, silver trays and golden candlesticks, caskets of jewels and sacks of coins. At last the butcher asked the king to come to his house. "Why, my friend," the good man asked, "do you give me such precious gifts? Look on my humble dwelling. Even if I were to live a hundred lives, how could I ever make return for all this wealth?"

Whereupon the king fell to his knees and told the butcher who he was, and begged to know the secret of the City of the Stupified. After an hour, the butcher sighed. "This very night, my king, you will know all that you desire."

When it was dark and neither moon nor star could be seen, the butcher led the

MINIATURE 6 *Bahram Gur in the Black Pavilion*

king out of the city to some ancient ruins where they found a basket encircled by a rope. "Sit here, my king," the butcher said, "and you will know why all the people of the city dress themselves in black."

No sooner was the king seated in the basket than the butcher vanished. The basket began to rise into the air, and the king was placed atop a desolate mountain tower. Suddenly, with a whirring of great wings, a bird of fearsome size alit beside him to share his lonely perch. Terrified of this colossal bird, but more terrified still that he would perish in that isolated place, he grabbed the bird's talons and when, at cock's crow, the bird prepared to fly, he was carried aloft through the still dark sky. At last, with the rising of the sun, the exhausted king found himself circling above an enchanted garden, where jasmine blossomed and rosewater flowed from a stream. He let go of the bird's feet and dropped into the perfumed paradise. All that day the king marveled at his flight and wondered about his future. When night fell, a company of lovely maidens, singing and holding lighted candles, came into the garden. They were followed by still more maidens bearing rich carpets and a throne of gold. Then there came into the garden a lady of such perfect beauty that the king was overcome by love.

The queen of the fairies, for these were magical creatures, ascended her throne and bade the maidens dance. With the infinite grace of birds, or leaves, that never touch the ground, they danced. Then one of the fairies found the king and led him to the throne. The queen raised her hand in welcome, but the king fell to his knees. When the queen asked him to sit upon the throne with her, he protested, saying he was unworthy of the honor. But at last he did as he was bid. All night long, until the sky reddened with the dawn, the king and his fairy lady feasted and drank; sweet dainties were brought, and fruits, and precious goblets of wine. Great was the king's joy, greater than any abacus could measure, and greater still was his passion. He showered kisses on his lady's feet and then upon her lips. But when he lost restraint and sought to embrace her, she drew back and gave to him instead one of her handmaidens.

And so it happened that each night a maiden would await the king—a maiden as delicate as the desert flower that blooms only in darkness and is most lovely when the sun goes down. At daybreak the maiden would bathe him and depart, and all day the king would sleep, fragrant with musk. When night fell, he would awaken and go to the queen and plead his love. But the queen would scold him thus: "Impatience is the vice of slaves, my king. If you would but content yourself with the charms of my handmaidens and ask for nothing more, all will be well."

And so, for thirty long nights, the king ached for the one who had denied herself to him. The following night, as a full moon rose, the king, able to bear his

Detail from MINIATURE 6

passion no longer, forced himself upon the queen. As he held her to his heart, she whispered, "Close your eyes, my king," and he obeyed. Then she sighed, "Now open your eyes, my king, to what must be."

He did as she commanded and found himself once again sitting in the basket, among the ancient ruins, with the faithful butcher at his side. "Now you have seen, my king, why all the people of the city dress themselves in black."

Then did the king return with his good friend to the City of the Stupified, and soon after went back to his own land. And from that time forth, the king dressed all in black.

The Yellow Pavilion

So ended the tale of the Indian princess. Bahram Gur sighed for the unhappy king and was well satisfied. "For a story I pleaded, my love," he said. "And yours was a story to make me bid the day of Saturn last for yet another day, that I might hear your wondrous tale many times again." And thus, with an embrace, they drifted into sleep.

All too soon, the sky was golden with the dawn. Bahram Gur arose and returned to his own chamber. It was Sunday, the day of the sun, and the king dressed all in gold. On his shoulders he placed a golden cloak, and on his head a golden crown. Then, with jaunty steps, he turned toward the yellow pavilion. "So sweet was my first bride, can the second be even sweeter?" he asked.

And the sun shouted in reply, "Yes, yes, oh king!" And there in the yellow pavilion awaited Humay, a princess from Byzantium. She was as fair as the sun that shone into the dome above; her hair was golden, and her eyes were flecked with amber. To Bahram Gur she offered golden bowls of fruits golden with ripeness, and golden cups of amber wine. For his comfort she brought cushions of golden cloth embroidered with golden threads. And all that day the king basked in her golden light. Evening came at last, and the heavens blushed; then did he make his request. "A story, my love," he murmured. "I would have a story."

And with a smile as radiant as the setting sun, the princess Humay began her tale.

Many years ago, in the land of Iraq, there was a king. Now this king had been twice blessed by fortune, for he had innumerable riches, more than could be counted in a hundred days, and he was the most handsome man in all the realm. Yet even so the king was not happy, for he had no wife.

MINIATURE 7 *Bahram Gur in the Yellow Pavilion*

Indeed, it was by his own choosing that the king remained unmarried. When he was a youth the royal astrologers had read his horoscope and had told him that in marriage he would find not solace and well-being, but incessant strife. Fearing that the astrologers spoke truly and that any woman he should wed would bring him only grief, the king resolved upon the single state. Yet his loneliness weighed more and more heavily upon him, until at last he could bear it no longer. He commanded that a residence be built, a palace of great magnificence and splendor. When it was completed, he bought the most beautiful slave-girls he could find and had them brought to his residence. With them he passed his nights and days. Soon he tired of the slave-girls and, without regret, sent each one away. Then, in solitude, he would wander in the palace gardens, yearning disconsolately for a wife.

Now it happened that among the king's servants there was an old woman, a spiteful and ugly creature, with toothless gums and hunched back. Her heart was as black as the warts on her chin, and her spirit was as twisted as her spine. For many years she had wished evil on the king, and when she saw him walking sorrowfully through the gardens, and heard his sighs, her pleasure was great. With malice, the old woman sought slave-girls even fairer than those the king had sent away. She brought them to the palace, enticing them with tales of the king's prodigious wealth. So fair were they that the good king fell in love with them all, and he gave to each a precious gift. But no sooner were the gifts bestowed than the slave-girls cried for more; they begged for robes made of the finest silks, and necklaces of pearls, and silver caskets filled with emeralds and rubies—treasures fit only for a queen. Such was their greed that they trembled and shrieked and wept until the king ordered the palace guards to carry them away. And again the king was alone, and he wandered wistfully through the gardens thinking of the joys of marriage, of which he was deprived.

As each day passed the king grew more and more somber. One day a slave-dealer from the far-off Orient arrived in Iraq. He brought with him a slave-girl of the most exquisite beauty. She was perfect as the morning star, and when the king saw her, he was overwhelmed with love. At once he resolved to buy her, and was greatly astonished when the slave-dealer refused. "I beg of you, Magnificence, take any one but her. In every country of the Orient, she has been bought by kings and princes and the richest merchants. But whoever buys her brings her back to me at sunrise the next day; the reason I cannot tell you, for I do not know."

The king's curiosity was as strong as his desire. Anxiously, he offered the slave-dealer so many jewels, so many pieces of gold, and so many other gifts besides, that the slave-dealer reluctantly agreed. Thus did the king buy the slave-girl, and take her to his palace.

Detail from MINIATURE 7

At sunrise the next morning, the slave-dealer waited for the king to bring the slave-girl back to him. The sun climbed, made its golden journey through the heavens, and at last descended to its rosy bed, yet the king still did not appear. Confidently the slave-dealer waited the next day and the day after that. And when yet another day had passed and the king had not come, the slave-dealer could only marvel at the king's good fortune.

Now the king and his slave-girl passed these days in pleasant harmony. All was perfect but for one thing. They feasted and sipped wine and sat under silken canopies or in the garden among the flowering trees; joyfully did they talk of love. But when night fell, and the king's passion burned, the slave-girl would draw back, and hide herself from him. At dawn she would show herself again, but when he begged to know why she had fled, she would only smile sadly and never say a word. At last the king became impatient. One morning, when the slave-girl came out of her hiding-place, he said, "Stay and listen; I have a story to tell.

Once upon a time, a long time ago, when King Solomon ruled the land, a son, an only child, was born to Solomon and his wife Bilqis. To their unending grief, the infant was deformed in all his limbs. He could not walk, nor could he lift even a crust of bread to his hungry lips. From the very moment of his birth Solomon and Bilqis prayed to God to send a cure, until one night the angel Gabriel appeared before them in a dream, and told them that if only they could speak the truth to one another, their child would be made whole. And so Bilqis turned to Solomon and told him that whenever she set eyes upon a handsome young man, her heart would ache with lust. As she spoke, the child stretched forth his hands. Then Solomon confessed to Bilqis that whenever one of his subjects came before him seeking wisdom, he thought only of the gift he would receive. As Solomon spoke, the child stood up and took a step."

When the king finished his story, he fell upon his knees before the slave-girl. "If Solomon and Bilqis spoke the truth, why cannot you, my love?" he asked. "Be not afraid, but tell me what you must."

The king was so gentle and so mournful, that the slave-girl could not refuse. She told him that it was the fate of every woman in her family to die in childbirth, and that she feared that she also in anguish would die; it was this dread that held her from the love of any man.

When the king heard these words, he rejoiced and loved her with all his heart. "Of all the slave-girls I have taken to my palace, you are the only one who was not greedy for my wealth," he said. "Indeed, I feared that you had kept yourself from me because I had not given you sufficient gifts." And the king presented her with treasures of unequaled splendor, as if she were a wife. Even so, when night came, the slave-girl still refused to yield. The king's rejoicing turned to sorrow.

The wicked old woman learned of the king's plight, and, at dawn, she went to him and maliciously advised him: "My king, if you would have this girl, you must first arouse her passion. Go to another; then she will burn with envy. So jealous will she be, that she will grant you what you wish."

Now it happened that of the many slave-girls the old woman had brought to the palace, all had been sent away but one. She was by far the fairest and had been kept in a secret chamber, out of the king's sight. This girl was as devious as her mistress, and every hour together was spent devising schemes to snare the king.

The king heeded the old woman's counsel and, when evening came, went to the secret room and passed the night, and the next night and the night after that, with the hidden slave-girl. Finally, she who had denied herself to the king was conquered by envy and at last, as dusk darkened the sky, yielded that which he desired above all things. With never a thought for the girl in the secret chamber, much to the old crone's great dismay, the king delighted in his love. The sun rose on their joy; the grass glistened with the morning dew; and the birds proclaimed their pleasure. And from that moment forth, of the king and the slave-girl whom he truly loved, no more is known.

The Green Pavilion

So ended the tale of the Byzantine princess, and as she told of the lovers' happiness, Bahram Gur was well pleased. "For a story I pleaded, my love," he said. "And yours was a story to make me bid the setting sun reverse its course, that this day should begin anew and I might hear you tell your tale again and yet again." And thus, with an embrace, they drifted into sleep.

But the sun was heedless of the king's command and soon darkness fell. When the heavens again grew light, it was Monday, the day of the moon. Bahram Gur arose and returned to his own chamber and dressed himself all in green. Then, with sprightly steps, he walked through a fresh meadow toward the green pavilion. "So sweet was my second bride, can the third be even sweeter?" he asked.

And the blades of grass beneath his feet whispered, "Yes, yes, oh king!" And there, within the green pavilion, awaited the princess Pari, daughter of the Tartar chieftain. Graceful was she as the willow tree and stately as the cypress; bracelets of jade adorned her slender wrists, and her eyes were greener than emeralds. When Bahram Gur arrived, the Tartar princess eagerly held out her hand and led him into the green depths of the pavilion where there was a garden. There, amid trees fragrant with flowers, they gave themselves to pleasure all that day. Evening came, and the trees and flowers of the garden shimmered in the light of the opalescent moon, and then the king made his request. "A story, my love," he murmured. "I would have a story."

And with a smile as gentle as a moonbeam, the princess Pari began her tale.

Once upon a time, oh king, in the country of Rum, there lived a man named Bashr, whose goodness was known throughout the land. Indeed, his charity was spoken of by all, for whenever any person was in need, be it a stranger or a friend, Bashr would go to him at once and give all that he could. Not only was Bashr charitable, he was greatly learned, and was as eager for new knowledge as he was for daily bread. And not only was Bashr learned, he was always mindful of God; he would meditate at sunrise and at sundown every day, and pray many times between.

Now of all his virtues, the one to which he clung most stubbornly was chastity, for never did he pay even the slightest heed to any woman, much less lose his head to love, or take a wife. Alone he lived among his books, and every evening, while other men delighted in domestic comforts, Bashr would study until his eyelids nearly closed. Then he would refresh himself by walking through the town, and afterwards he would resume his studies for yet a few hours more.

And so it happened that, one autumn night, Bashr left his studies and went walking in the streets. The wind rose and blew before him leaves that had turned golden and fallen to the ground. Through the leaves Bashr noticed a woman passing by. The wind, in a sudden gust, lifted her veil, and Bashr saw her face. Such was her beauty that he was stricken dumb; his limbs were seized with trembling, and he felt himself grow faint. Tears came to his eyes. Greatly alarmed—had love not been a stranger to him all his life?—he hastened home to his cherished books.

But Bashr could not study; he thought of nothing but the woman he had seen. He knew not who she was. He only knew that no rose could match the redness of her lips, and that her skin was white as milk. Despairingly, he shut his books and tried to sleep, but all night long he burned with passion. In the morning, weary and feverish, he rose from his bed. And all that day, he was distracted even unto madness; he neither ate nor drank, and had not strength enough to hold his books. He prayed to God, but the fever would not abate. For several days he suffered thus, until at last he resolved to make a solitary pilgrimage.

At the time, the moon was full. When again a full moon rose, Bashr had

arrived in the city of Jerusalem. He prayed to God in His own site. And as he prayed, Bashr's anguish seemed to ease. And so with gratitude and a lighter heart he prepared to make his journey home. As he started out, he met a fellow-traveler, a merchant who was also from the country of Rum, indeed from the very same town as Bashr, and they agreed to journey together.

Now this fellow, Malikha by name, was as unlike Bashr as night is unlike day, for as they rode into the desert, Malikha began to boast. He bragged about his knowledge, claiming that he understood the secrets of the universe as no other mortal could. "Why should I be as ignorant as an ox?" he shouted. "I have risen into the heavens, higher than any bird can fly, and have descended to the bottom of the sea, lower than any fish can swim. I have seen all, and at the mere snap of my fingers the wind will tell me when it will blow, and the rain tell when it will fall, and the sun tell when it will shine. That which ordains men's lives is known to me alone."

Thereupon the good Bashr shook his head and sighed. "These things, my friend, are known only to God. Do not speak so, lest He should hear you, and be angry."

"What care I for your God?" cried out Malikha. "Let Him be angry if He would!" And still he boasted, his voice echoing loudly for many miles around.

Thus did Bashr and Malikha travel across the desert. As they rode, the sun glared fiercely and the sand glittered with heat; nowhere was there shade. Nor was there any water. The two men had drunk whatever water they had brought with them, and as they trudged this way and that, across the burning sand, not a drop of water was to be found. Their thirst grew until they could no longer bear it. Indeed, they thought that they would surely die, when unexpectedly they came upon an enormous tree, its spreading branches thick with leaves. In the shade of this tree, sunken into the ground, was a large vessel filled to the brim with clear, cool water. From this vessel they drank like beasts, and then they rested in the shade.

"Praise be to God!" said Bashr, falling to his knees. "Praise be to God, Who has delivered us from death!"

"You are a fool indeed!" exclaimed Malikha. "Think you that God would put his vessel here to save our lives? A hunter sank this vessel, that a wild ass might drink from it and thus be trapped. Of this you can be sure!" Then he took off his robes, that he might bathe. Again Bashr shook his head and sighed. "My friend, do not speak so of God. And do not bathe, I beg you, for God's water is pure, and you are covered with dust."

But Malikha would not be restrained. So Bashr gently turned from him and walked toward the dunes. Malikha gleefully jumped into the water, but

Detail from MINIATURE 8

discovered that the vessel was really a deep well, and he could not climb out.

When at last Bashr returned, he did not see Malikha, but only his robes at the edge of the water. His heart was fearful. In vain he searched for his companion, in the branches of the tree and in the dunes nearby. Then he broke a branch, and probed for Malikha's body. He found him drowned, and in the shade of the tree Bashr buried Malikha and prayed for his soul. Then he took Malikha's belongings and continued on his way.

Bashr arrived in his own town, and after much searching found Malikha's house, and brought to Malikha's wife the dead man's clothes and possessions. And when he gave her Malikha's robes, he told her how Malikha had come to die. Softly she sighed, behind her veil, and tears came to her eyes. "May God have mercy on his soul," she said, "as He has had mercy on mine. I am relieved of a great burden, for Malikha was a wicked man, and most unkind."

Then she raised her veil, and Bashr saw the very woman he had glimpsed that autumn evening long ago. He loved her with all his heart, and took her as his wife. Thus did Malikha's arrogance cause his death, and Bashr's goodness bring him joy.

The Red Pavilion

So ended the tale of the Tartar princess, and when she spoke her moral, the king sighed. "Would that every man in my kingdom were as good as Bashr!" He was well pleased. "For a story I pleaded, my love," he said. "And yours was a story to make me wish the moon would never wane, that this night would last forever and I might hear you tell your tale again and many times again." And thus, with an embrace, they drifted into sleep.

But dawn came, and the moon disappeared. Bahram Gur arose and returned to his own chamber. Tuesday it was, the day of Mars, a day fit for a king. Bahram Gur put on his red cloak and his red headdress and, with bold steps, went to the red pavilion. The morning was glorious; the sun had just risen; the sky was streaked with scarlet, as if the very heavens had been set afire. "So sweet was my third bride, can the fourth be even sweeter?" he asked.

So buoyant were his spirits that he did not listen for a reply, but, with his arms widespread, strode into the red pavilion. There awaited the princess Nasrin, the daughter of the ruler of the Slavs. Splendid was she in her crimson robes; her hair was the color of fire and her skin whiter than snow. Her headdress was ablaze with rubies, but redder than rubies were her lips. And in the pavilion all was red—the roses, the wines, and the carpets and cushions on which Bahram Gur and the Slavic princess idled throughout that blissful day. At last the sun began its slow descent and the heavens burst into flame. The sky turned purple, and the king made his request. "A story, my love," he murmured. "I would have a story."

And with a glowing smile, the princess Nacarene began her tale.

Once upon a time, oh king, in a far-off province of Russia, lived a princess of unsurpassing beauty. So beautiful was she that in all the realm there was no man who did not love her. Yet the princess would not marry, for she could not find her equal. Indeed, not only was she perfect to gaze upon, but greater than any man's was her learning. So also was her strength and her skill with the bow and arrow. Moreover, from the strings of her lute she could draw songs far sweeter than any other musician, and with the painter's brush did she excel.

Suitors came to her one after another and, falling upon their knees, begged the princess for her hand in marriage. She would merely shake her head and laugh, and scornfully send them away, stating her resolve never to wed. When her father, the king, heard her speak so, he feared for the continuation of his line, for if the princess did not marry, he would have no heir to sit upon his throne. He pleaded with her to be merciful, and prayed to God to thaw her heart.

But the princess was heedless of her father's entreaties and grew more disdainful with every passing day. At last she caused a palace to be built high on a mountain plain. Then, with handmaidens and guards, she departed from her father's court, and to that lonely residence she went. Around the palace were towering walls of formidable height and thickness, and behind the walls were iron gates held shut with heavy locks and chains. On the road leading to the palace ambushes were placed, and these were so devised that swords were hidden in them. Anyone who approached the palace would have his head cut off.

Now in the palace there was a small chamber, apart from all the other rooms. Here the princess would sequester herself, from sunrise till sundown every day. In this room she painted a portrait of herself. When it was finished, she inscribed a poem above it declaring that she would give her hand to any man who could satisfy four conditions; otherwise, she would marry none at all. The princess would wed the man—and only that man—who was the handsomest and strongest in the land; who traveled the road that led up to the palace, and was able to escape her dreadful swords; who entered the palace by finding the secret that unlocked the door; and who could guess the answers to four riddles that the

princess would ask. All those who tried and failed would, without mercy, be put to death.

The princess gave the portrait to one of her guards, ordering that it be hung high on the city gates. This was done. The young men of the city saw the portrait and read the inscription. Undaunted by its dire warnings, they pursued the treacherous road. By the hundreds were their heads cut off. The king wept bitterly at their unhappy fate, but the princess was unmoved, and, laughing, had their skulls placed upon the city gates, all in a row.

Still more suitors came—these from other lands, for word of the princess' four conditions had spread far and wide. They too lost their heads, and their skulls were skewered upon the city gates. The king wept bitterly and begged the princess to end her cruelty, but all in vain. More and more suitors came, and the hapless skulls were piled so high upon the city gates that they could be seen for miles around.

Then one day, a prince, who was riding through the country on a hunting expedition, came upon the city. He saw the portrait of the princess. And from that moment he was overcome with love. When he read the inscription and beheld the skulls, he trembled with horror; tears of pity filled his eyes. "Surely the portrait must be magical," he thought, "for he who gazes on it falls under a spell. So even has the portrait cast its spell on me." Thus did he resolve to break the spell and win the princess for himself.

Now this prince was young and very handsome; indeed, he was handsomer by far than any other man in all the land. He was so fair and so graceful, that the sight of him caused maidens to swoon. And he was even stronger than he was handsome. He excelled at the hunt; whenever he drew his bow, the arrow flew directly to its mark, and it was said that with his bare hands he had killed a dragon. He could run more swiftly than a gazelle, and in the time it took the sun to make its journey through the heavens, he could swim across the deepest river and walk through the thickest woods.

But for all his strength, the prince was clear of mind. Thus while his passion would have led him to the fearful road at once, he went instead into the wilderness and there sought out a sage. "The princess has no heart," he said. "Thousands have died for her, yet she cares not. Tell me how I might escape her swords and unlock the palace door and answer her four riddles, for I must win her hand, that no more skulls be placed upon the city gates. Indeed, though she is cruel, I love the princess from the bottom of my soul, and for her I would gladly risk my life."

Now the sage was an old man; in his hundred and twenty years he had never seen a youth as handsome or as kind and earnest as the prince. "Death comes to

MINIATURE 9   *Bahram Gur in the Red Pavilion*

every man, my prince," he gently said, "but love does not. If you would have the princess, do as I advise." And he told the prince how to fulfill the four conditions.

Light were the prince's spirits, and quick was his heart with hope. When the prince went forth, he dressed in robes as red as blood, that all who saw him would think of the many suitors who had died. At daybreak the next morning, he set out upon the road. As he ascended the perilous road he plucked from each ambush its sword, until at last he came within sight of the fortress. Through its thick walls he passed, and through the iron gates. Leaving a trail of swords behind him glinting in the sun, he stood unharmed before the palace door.

Now the sage had given the prince a stick, which he carried with him. As he approached the palace door, he saw a drum, and with the stick he beat upon it, using many intricate rhythms the sage had taught to him. Suddenly the door opened. The prince entered the palace and found himself in a strange garden, where no flowers blossomed and no trees would grow. He waited there for many hours, until at last a handmaiden appeared. She told him to return at once to the king's court, and after two days the princess would come to him and ask her riddles.

And so the prince hastened back to the city. Upon entering the city gates he removed the portrait of the princess and bravely set about taking down the gruesome heads of his competitors. At once the people acclaimed him with tumultuous cries, for now the suitors' bodies could be buried in accordance with their customs. When he went before the king and told who he was and why he had come, the king embraced him and rejoiced and showered him with gifts. A banquet was set, musicians were called forth, and for two days there was such feasting and such drinking of wine as had not been seen for many years. On the third day, as the sky lightened with dawn, the prince was taken to a chamber to await the princess. Finally she arrived and proved more beautiful than her portrait. The prince grew faint with love.

"Ask me your riddles and I shall answer them, even on pain of death," he said. "For rather would I die than live without your love."

At that the princess took two pearls from her ears, and, with a lofty smile, she gave them to the prince. "What shall your answer be to such a gift?" she asked.

"May you live another hundred years, good sage!" whispered the prince, and he brought forth three pearls that the old man had given him. Then he called for a scale, and when the scale was brought, he placed all of the pearls on it, and the weight of his three pearls was equal to that of the princess' two; indeed, they differed by not so much as a hair. "If, as the scholars say, life is but two days long, here is your life and mine. And here is yet another life, which is our life together, when we are made one by love," answered the prince.

Detail from MINIATURE 9

Then the princess called for a mortar and pestle. When these were brought, she ground the pearls into a powder and added sugar to them. Then she poured the powder into a cup and, with a mocking smile, gave this to the prince. "What shall your answer be to such a gift?" she asked.

"May you flourish like a flower in the wilderness, good sage!" whispered the prince, and he brought forth a flask of milk that the old man had given him and poured the milk into the cup, and bade the princess drink. When she had drained the cup, there remained at the bottom only the powdered pearls, the same as there had been before, not a grain more or less, for pearls will not mix with milk and sugar. "So shall our love never be touched by anything impure," answered the prince.

Then the princess slipped her most precious ring from her finger, and gave it to the prince with a disdainful smile. "What shall your answer be to such a gift?" she asked.

"May your wisdom find its reward, good sage," whispered the prince, and he brought forth a single pearl that the old man had given him. Of the most exquisite perfection was the pearl, as luminous as the depths of the sea, gleaming and flickering in the light. For indeed, morning had passed, and the sun shone at the height of its golden glory when the prince gave to the princess this exquisite pearl. "As we give each other treasures, so shall we give each other love," answered the prince.

Then did the princess unfasten from her necklace a pearl that matched the prince's pearl. Alike were they; it was impossible to tell each from the other. And, with a scornful smile, the princess gave the prince this pearl. "What shall your answer be to such a gift?" she asked.

"May God bless you, good sage!" whispered the prince, and he brought forth a glass bead and a string that the old man had given him, and he strung the bead between the pearls. "So shall our love guard against evil spirits, that we may always enjoy good fortune," answered the prince.

Then the princess smiled with joy; she was as dazzling as the mid-day sun. And she wept with joy, for the prince had answered her four riddles, and had satisfied all four of the conditions. Then she bestowed her hand upon the prince, as she had promised, and there was great celebration throughout the land. At last the princess had found her equal. Thus the prince and the princess lived happily for all their days. And from this time forth, the prince always dressed in robes of red.

The Turquoise Pavilion

So ended the tale of the Slavic princess, and the king marveled greatly and was well pleased. "For a story I pleaded, my love," he said. "And yours was a story to make me dread the rising of the sun, for gladly would I stay another day and night, that I might hear you tell your clever tale again and yet again." And thus, with an embrace, they drifted into sleep.

But morning came, and Bahram Gur rose with the sun and reluctantly returned to his own chamber. Wednesday it was, the day of Mercury; the heavens were as clear and as blue and as smooth as a lake; not a cloud was to be seen. And in blue robes the king did dress himself and hastened forth, toward the turquoise pavilion. Swifter was he even than Mercury, as he thought eagerly upon the pleasures that awaited him there. "So sweet was my fourth bride, can the fifth be even sweeter?" he asked.

The birds that soared against the azure sky sang out, "Yes, yes, oh king!" For in the turquoise pavilion was the princess Azarene, the daughter of the king of Maghreb. She was dressed in blue, from her headdress to her slippers, and she had adorned herself with many rings and bracelets set with turquoise, and all about, in bowls glazed blue, delicate blue flowers put their blossoms forth. But bluer than the flowers were the princess' eyes. All that day Bahram Gur gazed into her eyes and lost himself in their blue depths, until, at last, night came, and one by one the stars appeared. The king then made his request. "A story, my love," he murmured. "I would have a story."

And with a smile as tranquil as the night, the princess Azarene began her tale.

Once upon a time, oh king, in the city of Cairo, in the land of Egypt, lived a youth named Mahan. Now this young man was so handsome and of such a cheerful nature, that in all the city there was none who did not wish him for a friend. And so, every day, Mahan would be invited to a banquet, and when darkness fell he would go forth to one house or another, and join his companions in the garden, where they would feast all the night and sing and drink great quantities of wine.

Now it so happened that one night, when the moon was full and Mahan and his friends were feasting, Mahan, blurry with wine and heady with the moonlight, wandered off by himself into an adjoining grove. There, among the palm trees, he saw a stranger who held out his hands to him. "I have been searching for you, my friend," the stranger said. "For I have just arrived from the countries of the Orient to find the gates of the city already closed, and my caravan, laden with precious goods, awaits outside the city walls. Under cover of darkness, I would sneak my caravan into the city and escape the notice of the guards, that I might pay no taxes on my goods. Help me, my friend, and you shall be my partner and share equally in all my gains."

The merchant took Mahan by the arm and led him deep into the grove. Mahan followed eagerly, wondering at the fortune that had come to him; indeed, he saw the very coins before his eyes, mounting like dunes of sand. Then the stranger started to run, and Mahan ran after him. All night long he pursued the stranger, but in vain. For when the sky turned golden with dawn, the stranger disappeared; Mahan fell exhausted to the ground, and slept. When he awakened, he found himself on a barren plain, under a glaring sun; around him caves yawned darkly and serpents writhed and hissed. Mahan shook with fear.

Gathering the remnants of his waning strength, he struggled on, uncertain in which direction to turn. All day he traveled in aimless ways, his fear the driver of his aching limbs, until as the light began to fail, he saw two figures, an old man and woman, approaching in the distance. When they came near, they asked Mahan how he happened to be in this desolate place. He told how he had met a stranger in the grove, and, promised a fortune, had pursued him all night.

"You have been deceived, my friend!" cried the old couple. "Know that the stranger is no merchant, but a demon, and that he has led you to a land where only demons live. If you would leave this plain, travel with us. But first we will tell you magic words, that you might be shielded from any harm that comes to you."

Thus they whispered to Mahan some secret words, though there was not a soul to hear them but the hissing serpents, and the three of them set out. All that night they journeyed across the plain. Then dawn came and the heavens lightened, and there arose a village in an azure haze. It seemed within easy reach. Mahan shouted and wept for joy, but when he turned to his companions, to point the village out to them, they had disappeared. And not another moment passed before the village also vanished, leaving Mahan by himself in a bleak and rocky gorge.

Now Mahan ached with hunger, for in all this time he had not touched a morsel. He dug among the rocks until his fingers bled, and gathered some meager roots, greedily devouring them. As he ate, he heard the sound of hooves. A man approached, riding on a stallion and leading a second horse. When the man asked Mahan why he was digging so fitfully among the rocks, Mahan told how he had met the old couple who had taught him magic words and led him across the barren plain.

MINIATURE 10 *Bahram Gur in the Turquoise Pavilion*

"You have been deceived, my friend!" exclaimed the man. "Know that the old couple are demons, and that their magic words are as worthless as these stones, and that the village is but a mirage. If you would leave this gorge, take up these reins, mount my horse, and ride with me."

All that day they rode, until at last they left the rocky gorge and descended into a valley. Strange it was, for although no one could be seen, faint music filled the air. Mahan became uneasy, and galloped far ahead of his companion. The music grew into a roaring din. Suddenly he came upon a procession of monsters more hideous than any creature to be imagined. Each had the trunk of an elephant, the tusks of an ox, and a hide of slimy pitch, and each carried in its mouth a lighted torch. The reins slipped out of Mahan's hands, and his horse began to sway to the rhythm of the monsters' howling. When he looked down, his horse had been transformed into a dragon, with seven heads, scaly wings, and a spiked tail. With a ferocious shriek, the beast flew from the valley, carrying Mahan aloft, until, at the cock's first crow, it threw him onto the ground. It bruised him with its scales, and raked him with its claws. When morning came, he found himself tossing in an exhausted sleep alongside a rocky road.

When Mahan awoke, he saw a light which beckoned him to a fruit-laden orchard. Now Mahan thirsted greatly, for in all this time he had not had even a drop of water. But no sooner had he plucked and eaten a juicy peach, than the owner of the orchard descended upon him from among the trees, shouting with rage and brandishing a stick.

"Indeed, my friend, you have good cause for anger," said Mahan. "Yet do not beat me, I beg of you, until you have heard my tale." When he told how he had escaped the demons, and the writhing serpents, and the seven-headed dragon, the owner of the orchard marveled greatly and shook the branches of his trees to shower fruit onto the ground, so that Mahan might gather all that he should want. And then, because he had no son of his own, he proposed to make Mahan his heir. But first Mahan must spend the night in silence. To this Mahan consented happily, and a platform was built, high in a tree. When evening came, Mahan climbed to his vigil.

Soon the moon rose, gently smiling, and there came into the orchard a company of fairies, together with their queen. They set a banquet in the moonlight, sweetly sang, and danced in honor of their queen. Paler than the moonbeams was the skin of the queen as she sat in the shadowy orchard. She was of such exquisite beauty that Mahan forgot his promise to the owner of the orchard and climbed down from his tree. All that night he stayed by the queen's side; they feasted on dainties and sipped wine and talked of love. When, as the moon descended, Mahan embraced the fairy queen, he found himself entwined with a monster of

Detail from MINIATURE 10

such hideous mien as to make him weak with fear. And thus he spent the last hours of darkness, enduring the unwanted caresses of the beauty now turned to beast. At the cock's call, which heralded the approaching morn, the demon vanished; the orchard was transformed into a wilderness, and the fruit trees became dead stumps.

Mahan wept with remorse, and beat his head against the ground. He now knew well that he had fallen prey to the temptations of the world. "Had I not followed the merchant, greedy for ill-gotten gains, never would I be in this wilderness where nothing can live or grow," he moaned. "Only God can save me now!" And he fell to his knees, and prayed.

Suddenly a man appeared, dressed all in green. Mahan was frightened, for he thought that the stranger was yet another demon in disguise. But the stranger softly said, "Fear not, my good Mahan, for I am Khizr, and I have been sent to you by God Himself. If you would be saved, trust me as you would trust God. Close your eyes and let me take your hand."

Mahan did as he was bid, and when he opened his eyes, he found himself in the same grove where he had first met the wicked merchant. He hastened to his own house, and there he found his friends, dressed in mourning robes of blue, for they had thought that he was dead, and wept with grief. When Mahan appeared, their tears of sorrow turned to tears of joy, and there was great celebration in the city of Cairo, and, indeed, throughout the land of Egypt. Mahan praised God and resolved that always, as a symbol of his salvation, he would wear mourning robes of blue. This he did faithfully and he led a life of goodness and was happy all his days.

The Sandalwood Pavilion

So ended the tale of the princess Azarene, and the king was well pleased. "For a story I pleaded, my love," he said. "And yours was a story to make me wish I could halt Mercury's swift steps, for all too soon does this night pass, and I would marvel at your tale again and again." And thus, with an embrace, they drifted into sleep.

But as the hour of dawn approached, even more swiftly did Mercury run, and with the first rays of the sun the king regretfully arose and returned to his own chamber. Thursday it was, the day of Jupiter, and Bahram Gur was dressed all in

MINIATURE 11   *Bahram Gur in the Sandalwood Pavilion*

brown. As dark as the earth were his silk robes, and his turban was as light as sandalwood. Then, with measured steps, Bahram Gur went forth to the sandalwood pavilion. "So sweet was my fifth bride, can the sixth be even sweeter?" he asked.

And the leaves of the sandalwood trees rustled in reply, "Yes, yes, oh king!" For in the sandalwood pavilion awaited the princess Yagme, the daughter of the Chinese emperor. Incense of sandalwood filled the air, and all around were unsurpassing treasures from the Orient—porcelains, carpets, satin and gold embroideries, and boxes and screens carved out of precious woods. And in the midst of these treasures was the most precious treasure of all: the enchanting Chinese princess. She was of such delicate beauty that the king was overcome; he likened her first to the porcelains, then to a butterfly, then to a lotus blossom, then to jasmine. Thus did he pass the day with his comparisons, until at last the sky turned rosy with the setting of the sun. It was then that the king made his request. "A story, my love," he murmured. "I would have a story."

And with a subtle smile the princess Yagme began her tale.

Once, many years ago, oh king, in a far-away country lived two youths, and these two youths were friends. Now all who knew them wondered at this friendship, for the two were as different as day and night. One was gentle and kind in all he did and said, while the other was harsh and wicked in his ways. Indeed, their very names mirrored their natures, for they were called Kheyr and Sharr, Good and Evil.

Now it so happened that Kheyr and Sharr decided to journey through the desert, to a distant city, and one morning, at the break of day, they set out together. As they traveled across the desert, the sun glared down on them relentlessly; the air grew stifling hot, and the sand shimmered with the heat. After a few days, Kheyr had drunk all of the water he had brought with him, and he thirsted greatly. "Surely, my friend, we will reach an oasis soon," he said. "I have not a drop of water, and my throat is parched with thirst."

"Indeed, I know the desert as I know my own right hand," replied the wicked Sharr. "And I can tell you that tomorrow we will come to an oasis and have all the water we might want. I, too, am thirsty, yet let us be patient, for tomorrow we shall drink our fill." But Sharr spoke falsely, for he knew well that the oasis was a week's journey away. That night, when Kheyr had fallen sound asleep, Sharr crept off by himself and brought forth a water-skin he had kept hidden from his friend. He drank until he was well satisfied.

Now all the next day the two friends traveled in the desert, and when the sun began its slow descent and no oasis was in sight, Kheyr fell exhausted upon the blistering sand. "Indeed, I can no longer bear my thirst," he said. "I can only marvel at your strength. You walk as if you thirsted not, yet you have had no more to drink than I."

Whereupon Sharr laughed scornfully, drew forth his water-skin, and gulped down the water. As his wiped his mouth, Kheyr begged him for a drink. "My friend, I must have water, or else I shall die!" he said. "In the name of our friendship, give me but a sip!"

But Sharr only laughed, and raised the water-skin to his lips. Kheyr beat his fists against the sand, and cried for water. Though his throat was so parched that his cry was but a croak, Sharr still refused.

Then Kheyr brought forth two precious rubies which he had hoped to exchange in the market of the distant city. "Take these, my friend," he said, "and give me only water in return."

But Sharr laughed yet again and tossed the rubies onto the sand. "What care I for your rubies?" he asked. "If I took them, later you will say that I had stolen them, and I will have to give them back. Know that there are jewels even more precious than your rubies. If I would give you water, I would have your eyes."

When Kheyr heard these cruel words, he trembled with disbelief and horror. He pleaded with his friend and kissed his feet, but all in vain, for Sharr would not be moved. Throughout the night Kheyr pleaded with Sharr until, at last, the sun rose and unleashed its fury once again. Then, with a heavy heart, Kheyr drew forth his dagger and gave it to his friend. "If I do not have water, I shall surely die," he said. "And if I die, then what use are my eyes? May you be punished for your wickedness, for your own light has gone out."

Sharr took the dagger, and when the dreadful deed was done drank deeply from his water-skin and spat in his friend's face. Then he gathered Kheyr's possessions, and the two rubies, and journeyed on alone, leaving the blinded Kheyr, half-dead and bleeding, in the burning sand.

Now it so happened that in the desert, not far from where Kheyr lay, a tribe of Kurds had made their camp. That very morning, the daughter of the Kurdish chieftain happened to be walking in the dunes carrying a water-jar, for she had just been to the well. When she heard Kheyr's moans, she ran at once to his side and gently put the jar of water to his lips. When he had drunk his fill, he told her his grievous story. The young maiden wept with pity. She put his eyes again in place, binding them with tender care, and brought him to her father's tent. When the Kurdish chieftain heard the tale, he sighed and shook his head. "Your friend is most wicked, and someday he will be punished for his treachery. But fear not, my good Kheyr, for I know a potion that will make you whole again."

The chieftain bid his daughter pick some leaves from the sandalwood tree that grew outside his tent. When she had brought them to him, the chieftain took a mortar and pestle and pounded the leaves into pulp and put it on Kheyr's sightless eyes. He ordered him to rest for five full days. On the fifth day, the young maiden said, "Open your eyes, good Kheyr."

Kheyr did as he was told. With shouts and tears of joy he found his sight restored. Then he looked upon the chieftain's daughter and saw that she was as beautiful as she was kind, and he loved her with all his heart. Thus a wedding feast was set. For seven days and seven nights there was great celebration throughout the camp. The Kurdish tribesmen wore their brightest robes and danced by firelight from dusk till dawn; banquets were laid, and there was much drinking of wine. When at last the seven days and nights of revelry had passed, the chieftain showered upon Kheyr gold coins and yards of silk and many animals and precious gifts, riches enough to last him all his life. Then Kheyr departed with his bride for his own country.

They had been traveling for several days in the desert when they came upon a city, and saw, to their astonishment, that all the people walked the streets weeping with grief. Kheyr, anxious to know the cause of this deep sorrow, inquired of a passerby. "Have you not heard?" the citizen replied. "The daughter of our king has been afflicted with a trembling in her limbs, and she will surely die."

Whereupon Kheyr went to the royal palace and knelt before the king. "Fear not, my king," he said. "For I have just come from the desert, and I have with me a potion that will make your daughter whole again." And he brought forth the leaves of the sandalwood tree—for these were among his precious gifts—and took a mortar and pestle, pounded the leaves, and bid the princess swallow the potion. For three days she slept as if dead, and on the third day she arose from her bed, her health regained, and left her chamber. The king saw that she was healed and, weeping with joy, offered her hand to Kheyr. Now the princess was as beautiful as Kheyr's first bride and so he took a second wife. A wedding feast was set; for seven days and seven nights, musicians played and wine flowed like a river. From the roof of every house banners of rejoicing fluttered, and every street rang out with laughter and the sound of dancing feet.

When, at last, the seven days and nights had passed, a high official of the court went before Kheyr. "Help me, good Kheyr," he said. "I have a daughter, and she has been stricken blind."

Then Kheyr brought forth the sandalwood leaves, pounded them, and bid the official put the sap upon his daughter's sightless eyes. This was done, and when the maiden opened her eyes, she could see once more. The official wept with joy and offered her to Kheyr. This maiden was as beautiful as Kheyr's second bride, and thus he took a third wife. A wedding feast was set, and there was great rejoicing in the city for seven days and seven nights.

When, at last, the seven days and nights had passed, Kheyr made ready to depart with his three wives for his own country. Yet so beloved was he in the city that the people crowded before the palace gates and pleaded with him to stay. The king offered to build a residence for him, with as many gardens and pavilions as he should desire, and to make him his heir, for he had no son. Thus did Kheyr remain, and he lived happily for many years. And when at last the good king died, the crown was placed upon Kheyr's head. He ruled with justice and with kindness, and the city prospered, and all his subjects were content.

One day, Kheyr was standing at a window of his palace looking onto the street below. It was thronged with merchants bringing their goods to market. In the crowd the king saw a familiar face. He ordered that the man be brought to him at once, and when the merchant came before the king, he spread his carpets and set out his goods. "I have come from the Orient but only yesterday, Magnificence," he said. "And I can show you treasures such as you have never seen before."

"What is your name, my friend?" asked Kheyr.

"Magnificence, I am called Mobashshar," the merchant said.

Whereupon the king trembled and turned white with rage. "You lie!" he cried. "Sharr is your name! You are none other than he who would not give me water in the burning desert, who put out my eyes, stole my rubies, and left me in the sand to die!"

Then Sharr bitterly regretted his wicked deed. He wept tears of remorse and beat his head against the marble floor. He kissed Kheyr's feet and begged for mercy. Kheyr at last agreed to spare his life, but he ordered him banished from the city, never to return. Thus was Sharr taken to the city gates, and turned out into the desert, still weeping with shame.

Now, for many years—indeed, from the very day that Kheyr had worn his crown—the Kurdish chieftain lived in the king's court, for the king loved him as a father. The chieftain never stopped thinking of Sharr's wickedness, and vowed someday to take revenge. And so, when Sharr stumbled past the city gates, the chieftain followed him into the desert; he drew his dagger and killed him. In Sharr's pouch he found the two precious rubies. He brought them to the king and told what he had done.

"Take them, my friend," the king said sadly, and he sighed at Sharr's unhappy fate.

Kheyr lived for many years more and led a good and happy life. From time to time, he went into the desert to savor the scent of the sandalwood tree. And always did he dress in robes the color of sandalwood bark.

The White Pavilion

So ended the tale of the Chinese princess, and the king shuddered. "May I never meet a man as wicked as Sharr!" And he was well pleased. "For a story I pleaded, my love," he said. "And yours was a story to make me wish that with the rising sun the day of Jupiter should begin anew, that I might hear you tell your tale again." And thus, with an embrace, they drifted into sleep.

But when the sun rose, it was Friday, the day of Venus, and Bahram Gur awoke and returned to his own chamber, and adorned himself in purest white. His robes were white as snow, his turban was white as a cloud, and in his turban he wore a white feather. Then the king went forth, with joyful steps, to the white pavilion. As he approached the pavilion the sun shone with such brilliance that the trees, the grass, even the sky, sparkled like diamonds. Bahram Gur delighted in the radiance of the morning, for this was the day of love. "Can my seventh bride be the sweetest of all?" he asked.

And the whole world shouted in reply, "Yes, yes, oh king!" And there, in the white pavilion, awaited the princess Diroste, a princess from a distant city in the land of Persia. So great was her beauty that Bahram Gur cried out in amazement. "To think that of all beauties, the most beautiful is to be found in my very own kingdom!" And all that day the king gazed with rapture on the Persian princess. She wore a white robe and a white headdress of the finest silk, and at her feet were pots of lilies and narcissus, but whiter than the lilies and the silk was the princess' skin. As the sky darkened with the coming of night, Bahram Gur's rapture turned to dread, lest in the darkness he should not be able to see the princess' face. So a taper was lit, and then the king made his request. "A story, my love," he murmured. "I would have a story."

And with a smile as fleeting as the light of day, the princess Diroste began her tale.

One night, oh king, in a far-off city in our own land of Persia, my mother was invited to a splendid feast, and at this feast she heard a wondrous tale. She told

MINIATURE 12   *Bahram Gur in the White Pavilion*

this story to me, and indeed it is this story that I tell you now. Many years ago, in that very same city, lived a handsome youth. Now this young man owned a garden, and the garden was so beautiful that there was none in all the land who had not heard of it. Yet few had seen it, for the garden was surrounded by four high walls, and the door was always locked. Every week, the young man would retire to his garden, sit beneath a tree, and savor the greenness all around him and the fragrance of the roses.

But then, one day, when he went to the garden, he found the door would not unlock. He heard music within and singing and laughter, and the sound of dancing feet. He knocked loudly on the door, beat upon it with his fists, and shouted with all his might. Thus did an hour pass; yet another hour. Still there was no response. Enraged, the young man took an axe and made a hole in one of the walls. But no sooner had he done this and crawled through the hole, than he was seized by two fierce women. His hands and feet were bound, and he was beaten and scolded for breaking like a thief into the garden.

"Know that I am the owner of this garden," protested the young man, "and that the door is locked against me, and I have been shut out!"

At these words the women untied him and soothed his wounds; they apologized many times over; tears of earnestness came to their eyes. "You have been wronged, and we ask your forgiveness," they said. "But surely you will look on us with favor when we tell you that this garden is a paradise and that beautiful maidens gather here, to dance and sing. You shall see all the maidens, and you shall choose one for your own."

Then the young man was taken to a secret attic room. Through a chink in the wall he could look down into the garden. In the middle of the garden there was a marble pool, gleaming with clear blue water, and in this water many maidens bathed. Around the pool, among the trees and flowers, many more maidens frolicked and danced and sweetly sang to the music of a harp. The young man nearly fainted with desire, and thought that surely these maidens were the most beautiful in all the world. "Each is more lovely than the other. Yet I must choose only one, when I would gladly have them all!"

For many hours the young man agonized, enchanted first by this maiden's blue eyes, then that maiden's golden hair, then the slim waist of a third, until at last his choice was made. The two women returned to the secret room, and the young man told them that he wished the harp-player for his very own. She was brought to him, and the two women withdrew. Such was her beauty that the young man wept with joy.

But quickly his tears became a rapturous smile. The maiden eagerly put out her hands to him, and he went to embrace her. And no sooner had he taken her into his arms than the floor of the secret room gave way. With a fearful crash the lovers fell, amazingly unhurt, onto the grass below.

"Do not despair, my love!" cried the young man. He led his maiden to a tree, and they climbed to a place where two branches met. "These boughs are thick and strong," he said. "Fear not, my love, for here shall we be safe."

The maiden eagerly put out her hands to him, and he went to embrace her. But again, as soon as he had taken her into his arms, one of the branches cracked, for a rodent had been gnawing at it, and the lovers were thrown, unhurt, upon the grass below.

"Do not despair, my love!" cried the young man, and he led his maiden to a corner of the garden. All around were trees and flowering vines; roses showered their white petals on the grass. "Let us make our bed of these rose petals," he said. "Fear not, my love, for nothing can disturb us here."

Then did the maiden eagerly put out her hands to him, and he went to embrace her. But no sooner had he taken her into his arms, than a family of foxes came running through the vines, pursued by a ferocious wolf. Trembling with fear, the lovers fled to the far end of the garden. The young man took his maiden into his arms. "Fear not," he said. "We will have time enough to know the joys of love, once we are wed. For surely the unsteady floor and the gnawing rodent and the snarling wolf are signs from God that I should take you as my wife."

And thus a wedding feast was set in the beautiful garden, and the maidens danced and sang before the young man and his bride. Forever after they lived happily, and every week they retired to the garden, to sit beneath a tree, and savor the fragrance of the roses, and talk of love.

So ended the tale of the Persian princess, and the king was well pleased. "For a story I pleaded, my love," he said. "And yours was a story to make me wish the day of love would never end, that I might hear you tell your tale again and again." And thus, with an embrace, they drifted into sleep.

But all too soon the eighth day dawned, and Bahram Gur arose and returned to his own chamber. Beautiful were his seven brides, each in her own pavilion like a jewel in its own setting; indeed, more lovely were the seven princesses than their seven portraits, and their tales were the most wondrous that Bahram Gur had ever heard. All that day he thought upon his pleasures, until, at last, the sun descended from the sky, and rose again in all its golden glory. Then he turned once more to his royal duties.

Now it was not long before a messenger arrived in the king's court bearing fearful news. The emperor of China had again amassed his forces, crossed the river Oxus, and invaded the land of Persia. He was pillaging the countryside

and laying waste many villages. At this news Bahram Gur became greatly alarmed. He ordered his army be made ready to march against the Chinese forces at the break of day, and he summoned his generals. But when they came before him, he discovered that his army was weak and in disorder, and that there was scarcely a coin in the royal treasury. "Surely this is the work of the grand vizier," he said, "for never have I trusted him."

Indeed, the grand vizier was a powerful and cunning man, for while on one hand he bowed before the king and kissed his feet and spoke many flattering words, with the other he emptied the treasury, and he greedily collected bribes from all who wished a favor. There was no man in the city, from the richest merchant to the most humble camel-driver, who did not fill his purse. Indeed, all the nobles of Persia lived in dread of him. And so it was that when the king asked his nobles what they knew of the grand vizier, the nobles dared not speak against him. But Bahram Gur's suspicions continued to grow.

Now it happened, one day, that the king sought respite from his cares by riding to the hunt. As the sky lightened with the rising of the sun, he rode into the desert, and there he chased wild asses until evening came. When at last he put down his bow and arrow, he thirsted greatly, for the sun's rays had been fierce. In the distance rose a thin stream of smoke, and Bahram Gur rode toward it. When he came near, he saw a fire burning brightly before a tent, around which were sheep. Nearby, hanging from the branch of a tree, was a dead dog.

At the sound of hooves, an old shepherd came forth, and when the king asked for a drink, he brought him water. After he had drunk his fill, the king asked the shepherd why the dog was hanging thus. "Know that I trusted this dog to watch my flock and was betrayed," the old man said. "This very dog became enamored of a she-wolf and allowed it to eat a sheep. Therefore I have killed my dog and hung him from a tree, although he was my friend."

When he heard these words, Bahram Gur sighed. "So have I been betrayed."

The next day, the king summoned before him all the nobles and attendants of the court and with them the grand vizier. When they were all assembled, Bahram Gur spoke harshly; he called the grand vizier a traitor and a dog and, trembling with anger, ordered him thrown into prison. Then the king sent forth a proclamation inviting all who had been wronged by the grand vizier to come to the palace to seek redress. By the hundreds did the king's subjects come forth, and out of all of them Bahram Gur chose seven to speak their complaints. As each man told his story, he was given just compensation. Finally, as punishment for his treachery, the grand vizier was hung on a cross, like a thief. And with the traitor's timely end came apologies from the Chinese emperor; peace and justice were restored and the country prospered once again.

Detail from MINIATURE 12

Now that his kingdom was once again secure, the king rode to the desert, on a hunting expedition. So swiftly did he ride that he left his companions far behind, as was his wont. Now it happened that a wild ass suddenly appeared before him. Thinking that the *gur* had come before him as a sign, the king followed the wild ass, and it led him to a cave. The *gur* entered the cave, and the king followed into its dark depths. When the king's companions arrived at the mouth of the cave in search of Bahram Gur, they could not find him. For many hours they searched, until the setting of the sun. And still they searched, until the sun rose and set again, but never did they see the king—that day or ever more.

COMMENTARY

The Seven Princesses

"The Seven Princesses" is the fourth and the most intricate poem of Nizami's *Khamseh*. Unlike "Khosrow and Shirin," it is not a tragedy but rather a bedazzling exploration of the pleasures of love. It fascinates as would a piece of jewelry made up of all the precious gems and brilliant metals the world has known. Though moral, for Nizami is always moral, it is one of the most intensely erotic poems of Persian literature.

At the same time it can be interpreted as mystical. Nizami is an enigmatic poet who does not draw a sharp line between the erotic and the mystical, and very often he uses one as an illustration of the other. This is one of the facets of his personality that makes his writing so compelling. The seven stories told by the seven princesses can be interpreted as the seven stations of human life, or the seven aspects of human destiny, or the seven stages of the mystic way. In fact, the title of the story, which in Persian is "Haft Paykar," can be translated as the "Seven Portraits," the "Seven Effigies," as well as the "Seven Princesses." The poem is also known as the "Haft Gumbad" or the "Seven Domes."

In Islamic cosmology, the earth was placed in the center of the seven planets: the moon, Mercury, Venus, the sun, Mars, Jupiter, and Saturn. These were considered agents of God, and in their motion influenced beings and events on earth. Nizami firmly believed as well that the unity of the world could be perceived through arithmetical, geometrical, and musical relations. Numbers were the key to the one interconnected universe; for through numbers multiplicity becomes unity and discordance, harmony.

Nizami used seven, the number that has always been preeminent among the people of the East, as the major motif of "The Seven Princesses." In Islam, seven is called the first perfect number. Combined of three and four, it is geometrically expressed as a triangle and a square. Traditionally there are seven seas and seven climes or geographical areas. Each is characterized by special physical conditions associated with the Body of the Universe and special psychic conditions associated with the Universal Soul. Each clime is symbolized by a planet which determines its color on earth by generating its own astral light. These colors are also expressed geometrically. Black, white, and sandalwood form a triangle: earthly sandalwood is the base, black the ascending side, and white the descending side. This triangle symbolizes body, spirit, and soul. The remaining four colors—red, yellow, green, and blue—constitute a square and represent the active qualities of nature such as heat, cold, wetness, and dryness; the four directions; the four seasons of the year; and the life cycle from childhood to death.

In "The Seven Princesses," the phantasmagoric movement of its hero, Bahram Gur, as he visits each princess, covers a symbolic path between black, or the hidden majesty of the Divine, and white, or purity and unity. The princesses and their pavilions are manifestations of specific planets, specific climes, colors, and days. The pavilions are domed, representing the structure of the heavens, the "heavenly bowl" or the "cosmic house," as it is often called. Nizami illustrates the harmony of the universe, the affinity of the sacred and the profane, and the concordance of ancient and Islamic Iran.

The number seven casts its magic spell throughout "The Seven Princesses." In addition to the seven princesses, there are seven portraits; a seven-headed dragon; a merchant who thinks he is a master of the number seven, who claims to know the secrets of the universe; and seven men unjustly treated by an official in the court of Bahram Gur. In the story told by the sandalwood-robed princess, the two protagonists travel seven days across the desert; and in the story told by the white-robed princess, blood boils in the seven limbs of the body.

Completed in the year 593 A.H./1197 A.D., "The Seven Princesses" was commissioned by and dedicated to the Seljuq prince of Maragheh, Ala al-Din Kurp Arsalan. The prince allowed the already famous Nizami a free hand in choosing his theme. Under the influence of Ferdowsi's *Shah-nameh*, which he ardently admired, Nizami chose an historical figure for his hero, the Sasanian emperor Varahran/Vahram V, known in Islamic history and legend as Bahram Gur, the "wild ass" or "the hunter of wild asses"—a favorite sport of Persian kings, for the beasts are clever, swift, and beautiful as well as strong. According to reliable data, Bahram was raised at the Arab court of Hira, the capital of a small Lakhmid kingdom, situated on the Euphrates and owing allegiance to the Sasanians. Emulating Ferdowsi, Nizami changed the geographic region where Bahram was raised from Hira to Yemen; it was not until the reign of Khosrow I, more than one hundred years after Bahram's death, that the conquest of Yemen by the Sasanians took place. This conquest is alluded to in the Koran, the holy book of the Muslims which also may have inspired Nizami to make this change.

Bahram's father, Yazdegerd I, was probably murdered in 420 A.D. by his nobles, who attempted to place an obscure line of Sasanian royalty on the throne. Bahram, with the help of his Arab friends, overthrew the usurper and ruled until 438 A.D. Almost immediately, as was typical when a strong king wrested power from the feudal lords, there grew up a host of legends glorifying his character and prowess. The Near and Middle Eastern people like their rulers to be mighty, rich, and handsome.

During his reign, Bahram Gur tried to unify the Persian aristocracy. The Byzantines were encroaching on the northwestern border, and along its northeastern frontier, Persia was threatened by fierce nomadic tribes. Bahram Gur gained popular support by containing these enemies and through tax reforms, spectacular love affairs, and daring in the hunt. He also excelled as a connoisseur of the arts. He was dedicated to music and brought musicians from India who were, according to some tradition, the ancestors of the European gypsies. Both the *Tazkerehs* and popular stories celebrate Bahram as the first Persian poet; he is said to be the author of the following verses:

I am that vengeful lion,
I am that mighty elephant,
I am that Bahram Gur,
My patronymic is Bu Jabala.
[The child of the mountain.]

The ruins of the Khavarnaq palace, where Bahram supposedly was raised, are located in what was Mesopotamia and were famous in pre-Islamic times and during the Abbasid caliphate. In "The Seven Princesses," Nizami says it was decorated with frescoes depicting Bahram's hunting exploits and that the Greek architect who built it wanted to construct an edifice which would change its color seven times a day. However, because Bahram Gur was cast in the role of exemplar of chivalry and heroism, there is more legendary than factual data existing about his reign and life. Even the accounts in the *Compendium of History* are shrouded by the veil of legend.

Ferdowsi, who in his *Shah-nameh* devoted some 2,600 couplets to Bahram Gur, tells that astrologers convinced Yazdegerd to send his beloved infant son, Bahram, to be raised at the royal court of Yemen. Four women, two Arab and two Persian, breast-fed the baby. At seven, Bahram began his formal education. A year later, he was presented with two horses, and, at his own request, a female companion, the beautiful singer and harpist Azadeh. He fell in love with her and made her his constant companion, even while hunting. The scene of Bahram in the company of a girl musician was always a favorite among artists. From the fifth century on, that is, shortly after Bahram's death, it was used as a decorative motif on gold and silver platters, and during the Islamic period it also appears on pottery, tiles, and in paintings. Azadeh is depicted as mounted on a camel or a horse carrying a lyre or a harp. Both Ferdowsi and Nizami would have been familiar with these artifacts.

Later, Bahram Gur returned to Persia, placated his inimical nobles, ascended his rightful throne, and fought against the Chinese—the catch-all name used for any invader from Central Asia; in the fifth century A.D. they were the Hephthalites. He married many wives; once while warring in India, he acquired the daughter of a rajah for his wife through his artfully displayed hunting skills. She is believed to be the prototype for Princess Furak of the black pavilion.

In "The Seven Princesses" Nizami, using the great historian Tabari (Bal'ami, his Persian translator and adaptor), and the oral tradition so popular among the people of the Caucasus as well as Ferdowsi as his sources, wove a poetic fabric of fabulous complexity and beauty. It is a treasure trove of Islamic stories. The history-legend of Bahram Gur is its framework, and both the introduction and the epilogue are devoted to it. They overflow with brilliant dramatic contrasts: the stars govern and so does individual will and ingenuity; the purity of desert life redeems the dissolution of the extravagant court; justice reigns and then is abandoned through negligence; but courage overcomes treachery, and jest, arrogance. All the frailties and strengths of human nature are illuminated by colorful stories and parables in this elaborate stage set.

The Fetneh story is an example; it is placed in the introduction and serves as an appetizer, anticipating the even more fascinating stories of the seven princesses. Fetneh, or Mischief, is based on the figure of Azadeh the harpist. In Ferdowsi, her story is related as follows: Once while hunting game, Azadeh asked Bahram to make a female gazelle into a male, a male into a female, and to pin with one arrow the leg of a gazelle to its ear. With a two-headed arrow, Bahram cut off the horns of a male gazelle, making it resemble a female. The double arrow then flew into a female gazelle's head and, impaled there, appeared to be horns. Instead of being impressed with this feat, Azadeh taunted Bahram; she suspected that he was assisted by demons. Enraged, Bahram threw Azadeh to the ground and trampled her to death under the hooves of his camel. Nizami changes and expands this account, giving it far greater psychological depth. Instead of being viciously killed by Bahram's mount, she is given over to Bahram's officer to be put to death. She persuades her executioner to spare her life for their mutual good and continues to tease Bahram, until he finally accepts her on her own terms. Fetneh is perhaps the most strong-minded, ingenious, and playful of Nizami's women.

But it is in the main body of "The Seven Princesses" that Nizami's full creative powers come into play. It is made up of the stories told by the seven princesses to enchant Bahram Gur. Each has been installed in her own paradisial pavilion in a specially built seven-domed palace near to his own. Bahram passes from one to another on succeeding days of the week, loving each and enthralled by each. There are stories within stories within stories, playing sensually on all the perceptions. The colors and ornamentation of the pavilions, the associated colors of the garments, the sparkling jewels of Bahram and the princesses appeal to the visual instincts. The continuous background music pleases the ear. The musky perfumes and the pungent incense excite the olfactory nerves. Taste is aroused by mellow wines and exotic foods, and touch by the finest silks and brocades. All these serve as aphrodisiacs, stimulating sensual desire. But Nizami, always true to moderation, tempers the erotic with restraint and hedonistic pleasure with responsibility to affairs of state. In spite of his delight in fabricating a myriad of tantalizing scenes and metaphors, the essence of the *masnavi* is that the physical passions are most preciously enjoyed when set in a context of virtue, simplicity, and kindness.

"The Seven Princesses" is written in the graceful *khafif* hexameter which scans as follows:
$$- \cup - - / \cup - \cup - / \cup \cup - // - \cup - - / \cup - \cup - / \cup \cup - /$$
Khafif means "the light one" and is very often used in *masnavis*. The poem is estimated to contain from 4,637 to 5,136 couplets.

J. Rypka, in his chapter on poets and prose writers in *The Cambridge History of Iran,* states, "In the tales of the seven princesses, Nizami's narrative art reaches the highest degree of perfection he ever attained. The most varied aspects of love are brilliantly conveyed, always with a profound moral basis. In his description of passion, Nizami commands the whole range from the utmost delicacy to the most extreme violence."[1]

The reader of "The Seven Princesses" receives the extrasensory impression that he is not only following the magic pen of a master poet gifted in the use of exquisitely formal language, but also a superb visual artist who works, though invisibly, within the reader's mind as he moves from story to story. He is enchanted by words that turn into living colors and shapes and is carried above and beyond the restrictions mere language imposes. This is the supreme power of a truly universal poet. Thus has the great Nizami mesmerized his readers throughout the centuries.

1. *The Cambridge History of Iran* (Cambridge University Press, 1968), vol. 5, p. 582.

Other Important Known Manuscripts of the *Khamseh*

Bibliothèque Nationale, Paris, dated 763 A.H./1362 A.D. (Suppl. Persan 1817, no. 1247). Described in E. Blochet, *Catalogue des manuscrits persans de la Bibliothèque Nationale* (Paris, 1928), vol. III, pp. 52–53.

Bodleian Library, Oxford, dated 766 A.H./1365 A.D. (Ouseley 274, 275, no. 585). Described in Ed. Sachau and Hermann Ethé, *Catalogue of the Persian, Turkish, Hindustani, and Pushtu Manuscripts in the Bodleian Library*, Part I: The Persian Manuscripts (Oxford, 1889), p. 487.

Bibliothèque Nationale, Paris, dated 767 A.H./1366 A.D. (Suppl. Persan 580, no. 1248). Described in E. Blochet, *Catalogue des manuscrits persans de la Bibliothèque Nationale* (Paris, 1928), vol. III, pp. 53–54.

British Museum, London, dated 788–90 A.H./1386–88 A.D. (Or. 13,297). Described in *British Museum Quarterly*, vol. XXXVI, pp. 8–11.

British Museum, London, dated 802 A.H./1400 A.D. (Add. 7729). Described in Charles Rieu, *Catalogue of the Persian Manuscripts in the British Museum* (London, 1881), vol. II, p. 564.

British Museum, London, dated 813/14 A.H./1410/11 A.D. (Add. 27,261). Described in Charles Rieu, *Catalogue of the Persian Manuscripts in the British Museum* (London, 1881), vol. II, p. 868.

Metropolitan Museum of Art, New York, early fifteenth century. "The Seven Princesses." Described in B. W. Robinson, *Ars Orientalis* (Smithsonian Publication 4298, 1957), vol. 2, pp. 383–91.

Freer Gallery of Art, Washington D.C., dated approximately 800–834 A.H./1396–1430 A.D. "Khosrow and Shirin." Described in Mehmet Aga-Oglu, *Ars Islamica* (Ann Arbor, 1937), vol. 4, pp. 479–81.

State Museum, Hermitage, Leningrad, dated 835 A.H./1431 A.D. (no. 23,001). Described in M. M. Diakonov, "*Khamse* Nizami 1431 Goda i ye Znachenie dla Istorii Miniaturnoy Zhivopisi na Vostokie," *Trudy Otdiela Vostoka Gosudarstviennogo Ermitazha* (Leningrad, 1940), vol. 3, p. 275.

Bodleian Library, Oxford, dated 841 A.H./1438 A.D. (Ouseley 304, no. 586). Described in Ed. Sachau and Hermann Ethé, *Catalogue of the Persian, Turkish, Hindustani, and Pushtu Manuscripts in the Bodleian Library*, Part I: The Persian Manuscripts (Oxford, 1889), p. 489.

British Museum, London, dated 846 A.H./1442 A.D. (Add. 25,900). Described in Charles Rieu, *Catalogue of the Persian Manuscripts in the British Museum* (London, 1881), vol. II, p. 570.

John Rylands Library, Manchester, dated 848–49 A.H./1444–45 A.D. (Pers. MS 36). Described in B. W. Robinson, *Persian Miniature Painting from Collections in the British Isles* (London, 1967), p. 94.

Topkapı Sarayı Müzesi Library, Istanbul, dated 849 A.H./1445–46 A.D. (H. 781). Described in F. E. Karatay, *Topkapı Sarayı Müzesi Kütüphanesi Farsça Yazmalar Kataloğu* (Istanbul, 1961), p. 149.

Topkapı Sarayı Müzesi Library, Istanbul, dated 850

A.H./1446 A.D. (H. 786). Described in F. E. Karatay, *Topkapı Sarayı Müzesi Kütüphanesi Farsça Yazmalar Kataloğu* (Istanbul, 1961), p. 149.

Chester Beatty Library, Dublin, ca. 1460–70 A.D. (P 141). Described in J. V. S. Wilkinson, *The Chester Beatty Library: A Catalogue of the Persian Manuscripts and Miniatures* (Dublin, 1959), vol. I.

Chester Beatty Library, Dublin, possible date 868 A.H./1463 A.D. (P 137). Described in J. V. S. Wilkinson, *The Chester Beatty Library: A Catalogue of the Persian Manuscripts and Miniatures* (Dublin, 1959), vol. I.

Topkapı Sarayı Müzesi Library, Istanbul, dated 886 A.H./1481 A.D. (H. 762). Described in F. E. Karatay, *Topkapı Sarayı Müzesi Kütüphanesi Farsça Yazmalar Kataloğu* (Istanbul, 1961), p. 151.

Chester Beatty Library, Dublin, dated 886 A.H./1481/82 A.D. (P 162). Described in A. J. Arberry, *The Chester Beatty Library: A Catalogue of the Persian Manuscripts and Miniatures* (Dublin, 1960), vol. II.

India Office Library, London, dated 894 A.H./1488 A.D. (no. 972). Described in Hermann Ethé, *Catalogue of Persian Manuscripts in the Library of the India Office* (Oxford, 1903), vol. I, pp. 595–97.

Soltikov-Shedrin Public Library, Leningrad, dated 896 A.H./1491 A.D. (N' 337). Described in B. Dorn, *Catalogue des manuscrits et xylographes orientaux de la Bibliothèque Impériale publique de St. Petersburg*, 1852.

British Museum, London, dated about 900 A.H./1494 A.D. (Or. 6810). Described in G. M. Meredith Owens, *Handlist of Persian Manuscripts, 1895–1966*, published by the Trustees of the British Museum (London, 1968), p. 66.

Institute of Oriental Studies Library, Soviet Academy of Science, Leningrad, dated 897–901 A.H./1492–96 A.D. (no. C57). Described in F. Babayev and E. É. Bertels, *Nizami Ganjavi Ikbal-name*, Azarbaijan Academy of Science (Baku, 1947), p. xix.

Bibliothèque Nationale, Paris, dated 909 A.H./1504 A.D. (Suppl. 578, no. 1250). Described in E. Blochet, *Catalogue des manuscrits persans de la Bibliothèque Nationale* (Paris, 1928), vol. III, pp. 55–56.

India Office Library, London, dated about 1500–1510 A.D. (No. 976). Described in Hermann Ethé, *Catalogue of Persian Manuscripts in the Library of the India Office* (Oxford, 1903), vol. I, p. 598.

British Museum, London, dated 946–49 A.H./1539–43 A.D. (Or. 2265). Described in Charles Rieu, *Catalogue of the Persian Manuscripts in the British Museum* (London, 1883), vol. III, p. 1072.

British Museum, London, dated 1076 A.H./1665 A.D. (Add. 6613). Described in Charles Rieu, *Catalogue of the Persian Manuscripts in the British Museum* (London, 1881), vol. II, p. 572.